OPERATION: BLOOD BROTHERS

Peter J. Atterberg

Local Author!

If you would like to contact me.

Email - peter.atterberg@gmail.com

Instagram - @atterbergpj

Thank You

Peterttark

To every soldier that has put their life on the line to defend freedom. To every person who has ever struggled with self-worth or self-doubt. To anyone who deals with the crushing weight of mental illness. To every person trekking for a better life. This book is for you.

ACKNOWLEDGMENTS

Life will throw us curveballs. It will take us on paths that may be dark at first, but then give us the strength to accomplish things we never thought possible. On those journeys you rarely ever do it alone. My journey is a complex story and one that cannot be told without speaking on the assistance of the loved ones in my life.

I want to thank my parents for always supporting me and my father for being a true inspiration for me. I want to thank a good friend and mentor to me, Jeff Siegel, whose counsel in life and in writing has been instrumental in the creation of this book. I want to thank my editor Matthew Meade, whose creative input helped me to create a better book than I ever thought possible. I also want to thank everyone in my life who has been a friend or a source of support for me.

Table of Contentsf

PROLOGUE

Fourteen-year-old Danny Richmond hopped backward, narrowly avoiding his father's front crescent kick. The kick came close enough to Danny's face that he could feel the air disturbed by his father's foot. He smelled the sweat in the room. He could hear each movement smack against the mat and echo off the walls.

Thomas Richmond continued to flank his son, offering a volley of kicks and strikes toward the boy. Danny was forced back into continual retreat because the next hit could signal his defeat.

Danny planted his foot against the ground. He shot his leg sideways and swung forward for a roundhouse kick. Thomas Richmond zipped his foot into the air and smacked Danny's leg.

"Come on!" Thomas shouted. "You must move faster if you are to hit me! Come at me again! You have desire and determination, but you lack focus!"

"But, father," Danny pleaded. "You are older and bigger than me!"

Danny's build was slim but muscular and meticulously defined. Thomas' body was replete with muscles that gave him agility and strength.

"No excuses!" Thomas shouted. "To be a true warrior, you must learn to take on opponents of all sizes! Your enemy will not go easier on you because of your size disadvantage! You want to quit? Then, Vincent, it is your turn!"

Danny stepped back into ready position. When he was not fighting, he stood facing the Thai symbols across the wall depicting desire, discipline, and determination. Light from the setting sun reflected off the matted floor. The walls were blanketed by shadows. His father's words struck anxiety and courage in him all at once.

Vincent Diezego stood across from Thomas and visualized his next move. *This is it! This is my chance to prove myself!*

Vincent and Danny were the same age and shared the same passion, but since Danny was Thomas' biological son, Vincent always felt the need to prove himself. Vincent placed his hands in front of him like a boxer. Each step he took toward Thomas was filled with anxiety. Thomas stood with his arms to his sides, fully relaxed, and eyes narrowed. How were either of them supposed to be able to get the upper hand on a veteran opponent who was not even concerned enough to get into a fighter stance? Thomas' move was psychological warfare.

Vincent screamed and charged toward Thomas, adrenaline propelling him like gasoline. Vincent executed a right hook, and Thomas knocked it away with his forearm. Vincent attempted a powerful jab with his other fist, and Thomas caught it with his hand like a catcher catches a baseball. Vincent yanked his arm free and moved in closer. Thomas was forced backward into a tiptoe retreat.

Thomas did his best to conceal the pride he felt. He was proud to see Vincent taking charge like he had been trained to do.

Vincent snapped a tornado roundhouse, and Thomas knocked it away with his forearm. Vincent attempted another roundhouse kick with his other leg, and Thomas simply tilted back.

Danny paid close attention to his father's eyes moving with Vincent's shoulders. *He sees Vincent's every move just before he does it.*

Vincent repeated the same routine of punches, with Thomas blocking each one. Vincent brought his heel back slightly, charging up for another roundhouse kick. Thomas' eyes peered toward Vincent's feet.

Vincent smiled. *Got 'em!*

Vincent exploded with a rocket launcher punch toward Thomas' head. Vincent's smile caught Thomas' attention. With a smack, Vincent's fist landed in Thomas' hands with a sickening echo. Thomas spun his shin into Vincent's ankle. Vincent's legs were forced off the ground, and his back cracked against the mat.

"You could have had me!" Thomas said, tiptoeing away from him. "You gave your cards away by showing me your emotions! You must remember to wear your mask while in battle, never show the enemy your hand! Danny, you're up! We will not stop until one of you manages to knock me down! Come at me!"

Vincent rolled over onto his stomach and stared at the mat with his fist clenched. *How? I was so close!*

Danny charged toward Thomas with the same aggression as Vincent. *I will make you proud, father!* The anxiety of failing to make his father proud was more potent than that of experiencing physical pain.

Danny exploded with a sidekick at his father's stomach. An inch away from impact, Thomas' hands knocked Danny's foot away. Danny sprung at Thomas with a roundhouse kick, and Thomas leaned back. Danny swung a left at his father that he blocked, then a right punch that was deflected, then another left punch that was knocked away, then an uppercut that was knocked down by his father's hands. Danny continued on this volley of punches while his father began to anticipate each move. Danny arched his shoulder back for another punch, and his father prepared to block it again and again.

Danny swung his fist forward, and Thomas threw his elbows up. Danny quickly squatted down and threw his leg sideways while spinning clockwise. His leg came barreling full force and swept into the back of Thomas' calves. Thomas' legs were thrown into the air, and his back hit the mat.

Danny felt pride and exhilaration run through him. He stayed faithful to his father's teachings and did not gloat. He extended his hand out to Thomas.

Thomas had the smile of a proud father while taking Danny's hand. Vincent was glued to the ground with a heavy feeling in his chest. He worked to hide the anger running through him. He came so close to besting Thomas, and then he failed. It gnawed at him in ways he did not want them to see. Once again, his light felt blanketed in the shadow of Danny's progress. *Why does Danny get it first every single time?! I don't get it! How is he always better than me?!*

Thomas, as usual, detected some of Vincent's turmoil.

"Why are you still lying there?" Thomas asked. "You fought very well. I am impressed."

Vincent shook his head. "I failed," he said. "I could have had you... I made a stupid mistake."

"Failure would be not trying at all," Thomas replied. "You are in training. You are going to make mistakes. Get up, and let's move on to the next exercise. I am very proud of you. You fought very well."

Thomas reached his hand out, and Vincent stared into his eyes. Vincent took his hand, and Thomas helped him to his feet.

"I'm proud of both my sons. You're becoming amazing young men." Thomas said.

CHAPTER ONE

The plane's engine roared with the turbulence of winds bouncing around the interior.

"Ready to jump?" Vanessa Rodes said as she kneeled behind a metal crate. Her slim but muscular build was covered by her military jumpsuit. At thirty-two years old, her every action seemed to ooze calm and intelligence.

"You know me 'Nessa. You say jump, I say how high." Danny Richmond quipped while reloading his pistol. The mileage of his life was written in the wrinkles across the forehead of his forty-one-year-old body.

They were two of the best CIA Operations Officers in the agency, and even that could not protect them from the winds that smashed against their bodies at fifteen thousand feet. The sounds of gunfire only added to the constant rumble. Sunlight blazed in from the plane's open door.

The pitter-patter of bullet fire sparkled the walls around them. Danny kept his head down while locking the harnesses of his parachute. Vanessa aimed her pistol at enemy targets at the other end of the plane. An enemy jumped up from cover to fire as she pulled the trigger. His body snapped backward, leaving a new stain of red splattered across his surroundings. Vanessa kneeled back into cover.

"Cover me. I need to strap myself in," Vanessa said. She tucked a stray strand of her dark blond hair behind her ear. She was as calm as if she were on a treadmill or hustling to make a departing train. Her expression made it clear that she was working out the scenario in her head. There was almost a smirk of excitement on her face.

Danny nodded and fired off a few rounds toward Lin John and the other eight enemies shooting back. The smell of the cool air did nothing to calm him from feeling his adrenaline and anxiety fighting to coexist. He checked a Velcro pocket on his vest. The package was still secure. It looked like a simple external hard drive, but the information on it could be a game changer in the ongoing chess match between U.S. Intelligence and the Xing. Danny knew that because the drive contained intimate knowledge of Xing bases and people, it made it desirable to certain decision-makers. The fact that it contained the exact location of a biological weapon Danny had hoped he'd never have to speak of again made the info invaluable.

Vanessa locked in the straps on her parachute and checked to ensure her altimeter was secure around her wrist.

"Do you have the files?" she asked, her words quick and terse.

Danny nodded. The mission had been *mostly* going according to plan, but here they were improvising again. It was their biggest strength. The Xing welcomed them onto the plane as potential allies. Somewhere in mid-flight, their cover was blown, and they had no time to figure out how.

The conflict halted to an eerie silence. The winds pounded into the airplane uninterrupted. A turbulence that nearly threw them to the ground came and went. Danny looked at his watch and his altimeter. *Fourteen thousand feet. Perfect altitude, I suppose.*

"We'll make a deal," Lin John called out from near the cockpit. "You two leave what you took from us, and we'll let you jump outta this plane. Square a deal as you're gonna find!"

In a few minutes, there isn't going to be any plane, Danny thought.

"Understand your situation," Lin John said. "You have killed Xings. Don't you realize what that means for you? There's still time for you to walk away from this unscathed."

"Fuck off, Lin John," Vanessa said, "How's about you all jump without parachutes, and we'll call the deal square?!" She looked to Danny, "I'm ready."

"Excuse me?!" Lin John said with a laugh. "You must realize the impossible situation you are in... Two likely CIA operatives are trapped on a plane outnumbered by enemies in a foreign country. You're both a long way from home…"

Lin John's uniform was decorated with ribbons and stripes from his decades of dedicated service to the empire. He and his men had been strapped to parachutes too. Lin John embodied what it meant to be a Xing. Victory at all costs in pursuit of the master vision. Lin had probably killed thousands by his orders alone.

"Danny," Vanessa said with force. "Whatever is on this damn thing is really important. Lin has never been known for his mercy. If he doesn't get this back from us, he's going to be killed by the people he answers to."

Danny bit his lip for a second.

"Hello?!" Lin called out.

"Just a second!" Vanessa said and then turned to Danny. "You've been hanging around that French model way too long. Her money's dulled your senses. We need to fucking go."

Danny looked at his watch again. One minute left on the timer. The less time Lin John's men had to follow them, the better.

"You jump first," Danny finally said. "I'll cover you."

"Perfect."

Danny leaped up and started firing. Lin grabbed the soldier next to him and pulled him in front. The bullets whiplashed the soldier's body while Lin dove for cover. Lin tried to keep his hands away from the splatter across his uniform. He ran his hands across his body to check for holes.

Lin John's breathing went into rapid speed.

"Sir! Sir!" The soldier Gerard cried as he tended to the wounded. "Carlos is shot, and I think it's bad! We need bandages!"

"Fuck him!" Lin John shouted with his arms out.

"But sir…" Gerard's jaw dropped, and he sat frozen in place.

Carlos struggled to breathe and looked at Lin John, who was frantically wiping the blood off his uniform.

"Stop standing there and shoot those two sons of bitches, you stupid idiots!" Lin John screamed.

"Sir!" The pilot turned his head from the cockpit chair and was now visible through the door. "We're nearing Colombian airspace! What should we do?!"

On the other side of the plane, Vanessa smirked, aimed, and fired.

"No! You idiot!" Lin John tried to bark an order, but the pilot's head had already snapped backward. Blood was stained across the cockpit window.

"No! No! No!" Lin John threw his arms around in a panic and screamed at his soldiers. "Get control of the plane!"

The plane started its nosedive descent.

A split-second later, Vanessa's gun was safely locked in the holster, and she was leaping out the door. Danny reached into his back pocket and produced an M80 grenade. He held it up performatively so Lin John could see it.

Lin John leaped up and pointed, "No! Somebody shoot them! Now! Now! They're getting away!"

Danny followed the same pattern only milliseconds behind Vanessa. He tossed the grenade across the plane's interior.

"Oh, Jesus, no!" Lin John leaped for cover.

Two Xing soldiers leaped to their feet, firing their machine guns as Danny disappeared through the door. Instantaneously the sound of the plane's engine was gone. The roar of the wind pounded against his body with a cascade of booms that sang out every second. The heat of the sunlight was dulled by the cool breeze of the air.

13,500 feet. Danny glanced at his altimeter.

Danny checked his surroundings. Vanessa was a safe distance beneath him. He was clear on all sides.

12,500 feet. He took another glance at his altimeter.

Winds fought to push Danny up while the overwhelming power of gravity pulled him closer and closer to the ground. Danny and Vanessa had their arms and legs spread out like wings in a flawless descent. They were in free fall at 120 miles per hour, terminal velocity.

11,500 feet. Vanessa looked at her altimeter. The skies were her arena. She had nearly a thousand jumps under her belt. She identified a small opening into the forest where they could safely land. From there, they would cross nation lines, and their backup would take them away to safety.

10,000 feet. Vanessa never went a few seconds without glancing at her altitude. 5,000 feet was standard for popping the parachute. That gave a jumper time to safely guide their descent into a wide-open drop zone. Their parachute pop would be at 2,000 feet, where they would glide into a thin stretch of game trail in the middle of a forest. The possibility of snipers made opening the parachute too early very dangerous.

A blinding flash scraped the skies, and a rumble loud enough to break through the wind followed. Another explosion had torn the aircraft to shreds.

There goes the plane! 7,000 feet. Almost time. She checked her surroundings one last time. Fiery debris could now be added to the list of dangers upon their final descent. She stayed focused regardless. Did Lin John make it out of that blast? What about his soldiers? She would have to troubleshoot that once they landed. For now, she had to focus on making it to Earth.

5,000 feet. Danny's focus grew stronger from the anxiety of going against everything he was taught about skydiving safety. The trees of the forest were growing larger with each passing second. The blended collage of colors across the landscape were transforming into defined paintings. The river became visible from in between the vast jungle canopy.

Beneath him, Vanessa's parachute sprung open.

2,500 feet. Danny reached for the ball hanging from his pack.

2,000 feet. He pulled the shoot. There was a series of clinks and the vroom of the parachute. His harnesses tightened around his body while the parachute sprouted into the air. For a split second, his body felt as if it shot upwards as the parachute fought against gravity. His descent went from terminal velocity to twenty miles per hour.

Danny grabbed onto the parachute handles.

"Holy shit! Here we go!" Danny shouted with a hint of excitement. What else could he do? He checked his surroundings. In the distance, fiery debris rained down. He looked upwards. Could he see his enemies still in free fall, or was that his anxiety playing tricks on him?

He knew for sure he saw the plane's shaft rocketing toward the Earth. He forced his eyes onto the drop zone. He had no time to focus on anything else.

Danny pulled down on the left handle and glided his body in a new direction. He then pulled on the right one to the same effect. The trees had become full size. He could see the breaks between treetops and hear the songs of mother nature throughout the forest.

He saw Vanessa glide into the narrow drop zone and disappear beneath the canopy. Danny pulled himself left and then right again into a swirl. All around him were treetops and branches that cloaked everything beneath. In the center was a small stretch of visible ground. His parachute was thirty-five feet in width, and to say the canopy's opening was any more than thirty-six feet would be generous.

The sounds of the air rampaging against the parachute seemed to grow louder as he came closer to the ground. The smell of rotting vegetation filled his nose as he glided beneath the forest's canopy. Danny raised his knees to his stomach.

The sides of his parachute ruffled against the leaves of the trees. He started swinging his feet until one foot after the other hit the ground. Suddenly he was in a sprint through mulch. Danny made quick work of detaching himself from the parachute.

"Danny!" Vanessa shouted, "You all good? Did you see Lin John anywhere?"

Vanessa was free of her parachute with her pistol in her hands. She ran to him while keeping her eyes everywhere.

Danny checked his vest pocket and could feel the hard drive still safely tucked away.

"All good here! No sight of Lin John. I have no clue whether he lived or died. There were other parachutes in that plane."

Danny was free from his parachute. They both ran into the jungle, disguising themselves among the trees. They felt the heat first. The plane scattered itself across the drop zone and beyond. The wetness of the forest contained the fire's spread.

Danny and Vanessa sprinted at full speed with their weapons in hand.

"Good job on guiding that jump, Vanessa."

"Thanks. We keep running?"

"Just keep running. The river is just up ahead. We hop on a boat and then take that into Colombia."

The Xings controlled Venezuela, and as long as Danny and Vanessa were in their turf of the Andean Forests, they would be cannon fodder. The Meta River could get them to safety. Only if they made it through undetected by Xing sympathizing Venezuelan soldiers and into the hands of Colombian guerillas friendly to the United States.

Danny checked his pocket for the hard drive and felt it slipping through a hole.

"I must have ripped my shirt on a branch. Can you take the package?"

Vanessa placed the hard drive into her chest pocket.

They heard the sounds of water and felt its breeze. Its smell nullified some of the rotting vegetation around them. They were close. Danny heard a crunch in the immediate distance, and he hit the dirt. Vanessa raced for cover behind a nearby felled tree.

The soldier shouted as he swung around a tree aiming his assault rifle at Danny. Danny fired a split second faster. The soldier went down as Danny rolled across the ground. His pistol went into his holster as he picked up the rifle. He kneeled behind a tree with Vanessa only a tree away.

Rifle fire pounded in their direction. Tree bark exploded into the air all around them. The songs of animals disappeared. The rifle fire pierced their eardrums, and it took away their hearing as a defense mechanism. Vanessa saw a soldier in her peripheral vision, flanking her position. She turned and fired at him. His body collapsed with another soldier jumping out behind him. The soldier tackled Vanessa to the ground and mounted her with a pistol aimed at her head. Before the soldier could fire, Danny pumped his body full of bullets. The soldier's body fell to the ground, and Vanessa grabbed her rifle.

"We're near the river!" Vanessa said into her earpiece as she rose against the tree for cover. "We've been ambushed!"

Danny observed the fallen enemy. He wore a Venezuelan uniform with the Xing insignia patched onto it. Xing fascism had been winning in this country too. It was another once-sprawling democracy that had succumbed to Xing fascism.

"Operatives," they looked at one another when they heard the voice in their earpieces. "Operatives… We can't get to you. Over."

Danny fired his assault rifle and sliced through two more enemies in the distance. With swiftness, Vanessa aimed at one soldier after another and fired. Three in a row went down. There was a reason she was called the fastest gun in the west.

And then, suddenly, it was silent again. Danny and Vanessa could hear nothing but the sounds of the river.

"Venezuelan soldiers with Xing insignias," Vanessa said. "I told you Xing fascism is spreading."

"Let's move," Danny said.

"Wait! Shit! It's missing!" Vanessa felt her pocket, and the hard drive was gone. Vanessa turned and spotted it just passed her tree.

"It must have fallen out of your pocket during the scuffle. No big deal." Danny said.

Danny left the cover of his tree, seeing no enemies in sight, and reached for the device. A tree branch broke nearby. Danny turned to the left while a woman wearing a Xing uniform stepped out with a pistol in hand. Danny made eye contact with her, and then boom!

Vanessa aimed at the shooter, but the splatter of Danny's blood against her leg froze her movements. Her eyes bulged open.

The shooter screamed and laughed as she sprinted away into the forest. Bullets rained down across their position and sent foliage exploding into the air. The hard drive had fallen even farther away.

Vanessa dropped to her knees and covered Danny to protect him. Danny laid like a pretzel across the ground. A pool of blood flowed from his head.

"HQ, we need backup! Man down! Danny is down!" Vanessa fell into a frenzy. "He's hit, and it's bad!"

"No authorization to go across enemy lines. Your primary objective is to get that hard drive."

Vanessa continued firing back at the enemies without time to react to the orders she had just heard.

"What?! Danny is bleeding! He's going to die! I lost the hard drive. Send a helicopter to come get us!"

"No authorization granted."

The words pierced into the deepest parts of her soul. *No authorization granted.* Vanessa had to make a choice. Either go after the hard drive and leave Danny to die or get Danny out of there. She wanted to be furious, and she wanted to scream, but there was no time to act on her emotions. Because more than anything else, she wanted Danny to live. Vanessa holstered her pistol and used every ounce of strength in her body. She pulled Danny out of the line of fire and to his feet with his arm wrapped around her.

His blood quickly repainted her clothes. She could feel him breathing. She could feel the warmness of the wound across the side of his head. After Danny's two decades of service to his government, they had made the call to leave him for dead. Vanessa carried him to the river. A boat painted with the Xing insignia idled against the shoreline. It would be what she used to get them to Colombia. If they wouldn't come for Danny, she would get him to safety anyways.

"Hold on, Danny, please." She said to him. *I love you, Danny. The world needs you, don't die.*

CHAPTER TWO

Vanessa sat inside a Colombian hospital with her head buried in her hands. *No authorization granted.* The coldness of the words hissed like acid in her memory. How was it possible? After Danny's two decades of service... *No authorization granted.*

Vanessa rubbed her temple. A TV near her blared with breaking news. The Colombian news anchor went on about a deadly plane crash near the Colombian-Venezuelan border. It was being dubbed as another conflict between both countries.

The lobby around her was far calmer than she was on the inside. A family sat together, waiting on results. A few patients sat there alone, scrolling through their phones. Vanessa checked her front pants pocket. *The hard drive is gone too.* Vanessa found herself stricken with terrible guilt. She lost the hard drive, and Danny got shot trying to fix her mistake. If she had just reacted faster, then perhaps Danny would have been okay. She envisioned the alternate timeline where she shot both enemies trying to tackle her. They would be on their way to Langley with a mission accomplished, and nobody hurt.

"What's the status on the device, Officer Rodes?" She remembered the Chief of Station asking over the phone. Danny Richmond's fate was their *second* question. Even though she knew the rules of the game, that still ate at her.

A door opened, and she snapped her head up.

"Jimenez family?" The nurse asked.

Damn it, she thought to herself. She stood up and walked over to the window overlooking the city. *How the fuck could they just leave Danny? How could I let him get shot?*

The television caught Vanessa's ear, and she looked toward it. The news anchor spoke over images of well-dressed politicians smiling daggers at each other.

"Venezuelan President Abiezer Ramero officially shook hands with the head of now ruling People's Freedom Movement," the news anchor explained. "President Ramero stated in his address he looked forward to what the Xing-influenced party and his administration could do to save Venezuelans from Western intrusion, mass hunger, and government corruption in Venezuela."

Another country fallen. Vanessa thought with a heavy heart.

"Vanessa?"

She looked up, and the doctor waved her over. Vanessa followed the doctor to a room. The doctor was young but already looked worn out from the endless torrent of bad news she had to give families.

"Give it to me straight, doc," Vanessa said, making sure to speak Spanish in the Colombian dialect to ensure the doctor gave her all the information about Danny and not just the broad strokes.

"He'll be fine, eventually."

"Eventually?"

"The bullet sliced through the tip of his skull. It never touched his brain. He may have a scar on the back of his head, but that's it. However, he fell into a shock which has put him into a coma. We think he'll awaken soon."

Vanessa's chest constricted, and her eyes watered. Her hand shook rapidly. No amount of training could give her the tools needed to hide her panic.

"A… a coma?" She said, "How? You said the bullet never even hit his brain!"

"Well," the doctor put her hand on Vanessa's shoulder, "He went into shock. That is what got him. I'm so sorry. We can treat him here. How long did you say your hotel was good for?"

"Another two weeks," Vanessa said without missing a beat.

"I'm sorry your guys' vacation turned out this way. Crime is getting bad everywhere. Please, go back to your hotel, get some rest. There's nothing more you can do for him right now. We can call you if anything changes."

"Thank you, doctor."

"Do you need anything else?"

"No. Thank you. I think I would like to be alone now."

The doctor walked away. Vanessa took a deep breath to bury what she was feeling on the inside. She stepped out the doorway. She looked toward the exit to the lobby where she was expected to go and then took a look down the hallway leading to Danny. Vanessa turned toward Danny and marched over.

Vanessa stopped at the doorway of Danny's room. *Keep it steady.* She walked in. The EKG machines confirmed life with every beep. The sounds of the hustle and bustle of medical staff in the hallway spilled into the room. A musky hospital smell lingered in the air.

She thought she could hear Danny's breathing. She knew she could see the bandage across his forehead. The overcast skies through the window cast a gray haze across the room. Danny lay on the hospital bed with both eyes closed. His chest rose and fell with each breath. There was no other movement. The powerful Danny Richmond, who had been responsible for saving democracy, was silent. Hours ago, he would have been considered one of the deadliest martial artists in the world. Now, he was helpless, and she felt at fault.

Vanessa's hands started to tremble, and her knees grew weak. There it was: the panic. She raced to bury it by redirecting her thoughts and focusing on her breathing. Her hands trembled anyways. Her legs gave out, and her knees met the floor. Vanessa grabbed onto Danny's wrist, squeezing as tightly as possible.

A tear escaped her eye. Her breathing grew heavier. Another tear escaped with her foot shaking.

"D-Danny...No..." She gasped, "Danny...Come on...No..."

He was supposed to be the best. He had been hit with bullets many times before. Each time he made a quick recovery and got back in action.

"I…" Her lips quivered, "I love you, Danny…" There, she said it. What she truly felt about him for over a decade. It was the true feelings she never properly expressed to him. She knew deep down that he felt the same. It was their open secret that they never dared to talk about. He was her best friend. She was known as the *most* efficient Operations Officer. Even more so than Danny. Where he would sometimes allow his ego to make his decisions for him, she would stay calm and calculated.

They completed each other in the field. In their private lives, they kept each other sane. They were each other's rock. Danny had a key to her condo, and she had a key to his house. Danny was Vanessa's loudest cheerleader. He never missed a moment to remind her how intelligent she was, how good of a fighter she was or how good of a heart she had. Yet, their love lives never crossed. Was it going to be too late now?

Vanessa took another deep breath. *Remember your training.* She rose to her feet and pulled up a chair. She sat down and fell victim to her own thoughts. What happens to the world? What about the Xings? What of this device they lost? What would happen with all of that now? No matter what, she knew she was going to update the agency with the truth. It's what Danny would have done. It's what she would do. Democracy had to come first, right?

Vanessa took one more look at Danny and took his hand. She knew her new mission was to protect Danny at all costs. She held it firmly and stared out the window, letting her thoughts run freely. The love of her life was in a bad way, and whether she liked it or not, the fate of the world hung in the balance.

CHAPTER THREE

The post-work-out sweat was still trailing down Danny's face. He walked through the halls of his magnificent house in Winnetka, Illinois. One of the wealthiest cities in the state. It had been two years since the mission in Venezuela, and he had not been on a mission since.

His continued relationship with Maryse and his employment in Wall Street Day trading had afforded him this beautiful home. His body looked as fit as ever. The black bags that had once laid claim under his eyes were gone. His skin was smooth, and his Giorgio Armani suit decked out to near perfection. Yet, underneath all of that bluster were inescapable nerves.

Danny opened the front door.

"Danny," Vanessa said with a smile, "It's so good to finally see you."

She stepped in, and he closed the door behind her. They embraced in a tight hug that didn't last long enough for either of them.

She was in jeans and a tank top.

Danny turned around, and his gold Rolex glistened in the sunlight.

Vanessa glared at the watch and the house all around her.

"This place is like a fuckin' mansion..." Vanessa remarked with her jaw dropped. It was in stark contrast to the type of house she grew up in.

"How do you like it?" Danny asked.

"How have you been, Danny?" Vanessa stared into his eyes. It was clear she was eying him up as he was her.

"Why?" Danny gulped

Vanessa paused for a moment, and Danny knew what was on her mind.

"Why are you asking?"

Vanessa took a deep breath. "How are you doing?"

"Really well, actually. I'm feelin' good… Relaxed." Danny smiled widely, "I'm gaining new perspectives. I'm back to running a lot of miles. I'm walking again. I have you to thank for helping me through that process. Hell, I'd dare say I'm fully recovered now. Things are going well with my girlfriend, Maryse."

Danny was forever in debt to how dedicated Vanessa was to seeing him through the first steps of his recovery. No matter how long it had been since they had seen each other, he would never forget what she did for him. He literally had to learn to walk all over again when he awoke from his coma, and Vanessa was with him daily during that process.

"You're walking really well. In fact, you'd never even know." Her eyes widened. The softness of her smile showed how genuinely happy she was for him.

"Doctor said I'm fully recovered in that area!" Danny remarked with a fist pump, "Care for a drink?"

"Please."

Danny showed her around the house on the way to the kitchen. An hour had passed, and they were standing in the kitchen across from each other. They were both in mid-laughter.

Danny put his drink down.

"Vanessa. I really do want to thank you for seeing me through. Those first few months after I woke up were terrifying."

"Eleven years ago, we made a pact. A pact that we would always have each other's back. I meant it when I said it. You showed so much damn courage in those moments. No amount of training could have prepared for us that, and yet you pulled through."

Danny nodded.

"It's been a long year and a half without seeing you," he said. "The texts and letters were great, but I missed you. A lot. Let's get real now. How have *you* been doing? No wounds? All your allies make it back okay? New enemies or more of the same?"

"Well," Vanessa put her drink down, "All my allies made it back alive. I've been on a few missions. Some bore more fruit than others. Enemies have gotten stronger and multiplied. Things are getting worse."

"Look…" She leaned toward him and took a deep breath. "There's something I need to say to you. I know it was hard for you when I went back… However, I had to. When I took that oath with the agency, I did it for all the right reasons. We were on the lead to something huge that I couldn't stay away from. It was eating away at me. As I got more reports of what was on that hard drive I lost. I couldn't wait around any longer."

Vanessa ran her hand through her hair. Her eyes never left Danny's.

"I don't ever want you to carry that burden. When I woke up, you helped teach me how to fuckin' walk again," Danny raised his eyebrows, "I can't lie to you and say recovery has been a breeze; it hasn't been. But I know damn well what you had to do, and you know damn well I support it. The show had to go on. That's how the game is. I knew that going into it. Country and the needs of the many first."

Vanessa took another deep breath, "The show did have to go on, which brings me to why I'm here. I didn't just come here to make sure you were doing okay and to catch up. I also came here on business."

Danny walked away without saying a word. He shook his head while turning into the hallway.

"Wait, Danny!" Vanessa said as she followed him. "Will you stop for a second?"

Danny kept marching forward. Vanessa grabbed him by the shoulder.

"Damn it!" she said. "Will you stop just for just one second?!"

"Me stop?" He halted and pointed at her, "What about you? Do you realize exactly what you just asked of me?"

"Danny you gotta go back. It's just as a consulting position in the office, behind a desk. You wouldn't even be on the field or need to carry a gun. Look, I have new intelligence on the Xings. That hard drive had a lot of really seriously dangerous shit in it."

"What about your other partners?" He asked with a squint. It was a façade to hide his anxiety.

"They're not you. They don't have the contacts you do. They don't know the game like you do."

"Alright, then who sent you to come get me? Was it somebody from the seventh floor at Langley?"

"Excuse me? Nobody in senior management ordered me here. I came here on my own accord. The folks in the Counterterrorism Center miss you. I miss you. And to be honest, I feel safer when I know you're by my side."

"Vanessa, I can't help you. I'm sorry…I'm not that guy anymore…"

Vanessa looked up and down at him. She looked at his gold watch and his suit.

"Now what? Why are you looking at my clothes? You don't like this outfit?" Danny saw it instantly.

"No, it's just that, well—Well fuck it. You'll say no to a mission, but yes to all of this? Danny, is this you?"

"What do you mean?" Danny said. "Is what me? Because I'm dressin' with a little bit of fashion all of a sudden, I've got problems? I just told you everything was fine with me. I'm fully recovered!"

"You say you're fully recovered, and yet you haven't been on a mission in—"

His eyes widened, but he tried to keep his poker face on. A near-impossible task around Vanessa. He hoped she couldn't detect his heartbeat picking up and the sinking feeling in his shoulders.

"Really? We're going to keep going low like that? You just walked in the door, and now this. How's about we go cook up dinner and talk about our weekend plans." He waved her off and kept walking. His smile appeared forced. He opened the balcony door and stepped out.

Vanessa bit her lip and followed him onto the balcony. The sun shined brightly across their bodies. Birds and butterflies hovered around the plants hanging off the concrete railings. The air's cool breeze and the warm temperature mixed perfectly together.

Danny turned around and saw Vanessa standing in the sunlight. Suddenly the mood changed. *There, that stance. She is so fucking intelligent.* Danny could not keep his eyes off of her eyes. They were intoxicating to him, and yet he felt powerless to tell her.

The seriousness of their conversation suddenly vanished. Now it was just Danny and his own emotions. He didn't know how he would feel seeing Vanessa again because something had changed for him two years ago. He saw Vanessa so much more clearly than he had allowed himself to in the past.

Vanessa stood across from him on the balcony. She wanted to focus on the task at hand, and yet this moment stole away her concentration. His eyes bore into her soul, and she found them intoxicating. *There he is again with those fuck me eyes. Just fuckin' take me already.*

"Danny..." she wanted to be serious, but his nonchalant demeanor with the sun gazing across his body forced a smile out of her. Something changed for her two years ago too. She had almost lost Danny without either of them ever speaking the truth. Maybe it was time to break the silence. Say something. Such a long time without seeing him had changed her perspective. She had forgotten just how attracted to him she was. Just how strong her emotions were for him.

Danny pulled out his phone and connected its Bluetooth to the balcony radio. Beethoven's Ode to Joy started playing at a quiet level. Danny sat down on the edge of a long chair. The time apart made him love her even more. He had forgotten just how beautiful she was.

"Come on, sit down," he said.

Vanessa sat across from him.

"Do you realize it's been eleven years since we met?" Danny asked.

"Has it already been eleven years? Jesus…" She wanted to get closer, but the reality was Maryse could walk in at any moment. "Where does the time go? Feels like just yesterday I was walking into Langley for the first time. Fresh out of the Air Force. Things were so much different back then."

Danny seriously thought about telling her. But how could he? He was committed to someone else. And what of the past? What if Vanessa got hurt?

Vanessa stared at him again. *Kiss me, you fuckin' idiot. I forgot how much I wanted you.*

Danny stared back at her. *Oh fuck. She is just a fuckin' fox.*

Danny let himself quickly daydream about a different world where they were an item. What would that look like? He knew Vanessa must be wondering the same thing.

"It's been two years now," Vanessa said, waking Danny up from his daydream. The look on her face brought the serious conversation back into focus.

Danny rose from his seat and walked over to the balcony, "And so it has…" His smile was gone. In his mind, the plane was exploding all over again. He was freefalling at 120 miles per hour. The rest he could only remember through his vest's camera. The look in his shooter's eyes. The joyous grin across her face as she fired the bullet. His body tumbling backward, and Vanessa's panic.

He heard the recording in his head. *No authorization granted.*

"Listen," Vanessa stood up. "The world needs us. It's just a desk role. I really think it would give you a purpose again."

Danny continued looking across the horizon.

"Things have gotten much worse," Vanessa said. "Xings are a threat not just to the United States, but to democracy worldwide. Their fascist ideology is spreading like a virus. Do you remember the name Xing Lei?"

"Of course, I do. I haven't forgotten everything. He's the ruler of the Xing Empire. He is their dictator."

"Yea, well, he's been more active than ever before. He's been killing a lot too. All the Xings have been. Something big is coming. You and I were on the trail of it before we left. We have resources others don't have. People that will only speak to us. We need to start back where we left off. Get back into the fight. Find that hard drive too."

"Why now?" Danny looked to her. "Look, if you ask me, the Xings ain't that big of a threat. The world's still turning, ain't it? Democracy hasn't crumbled. Roads are still being repaired; life is going on. Hell, it'll pass like it always does. If the situation were that bad, our government would already be pulling out all the stops to get a handle on it."

Danny tapped his fist against the cement railing, "Everything's fine. The agency has plenty of other capable operatives."

"The fuck did you just say? The agency has other capable agents? The Danny I knew would rush to go in and resolve the crisis himself." Vanessa threw her arms out. "That hard drive had the exact location of the biological weapon. The DLX."

The flashbacks of his shooter were bad enough. The screams from his very first special assignment compounded his racing heart and the pinching sensation in his chest. He could see the dead bodies as if they were in front of him.

"N-No…" he muttered under his breath, "The DLX?"

"Yes…"

"Doesn't mean anything. The government would have moved it in time."

"I got word the DLX went missing a week ago."

"To where?"

"How the hell should I know?" Vanessa squinted, "But that's not a coincidence."

"No," Danny shook his head, "Listen to me, a weapon like that is so heavily protected. You'd need the highest security clearance available. Want to know what I think happened?"

"Enlighten me," she said with a sarcastic tone.

"I think someone heard the Xings were after the weapon and decided to destroy it for the betterment of humanity. They did what Vincent, Selena, and I should have done during the war when we retrieved it. As for the hard drive, what's it matter?"

"Cut the bullshit, Danny!" Vanessa shouted. "You can't really believe that!"

"You're damn right I can! Don't forget I got an additional ten years of experience on you in this game. I know how this shit works."

"I know how this shit works too. I also know what's going on with you. I mean, look at this. Fancy houses, gold watches, and exotic cars? That's not you. You never gave a crap about any of this stuff before. It started when you got with Maryse, and then it got worse since your accident."

"I happen to love Maryse. So, there's that. Her having money doesn't make me any less of who I was. It doesn't mean I'm unhealthy."

Vanessa paused and stared into Danny's eyes differently than earlier. Danny could feel her concern.

"Earlier you said you made a full recovery. If that's true, then how's your memory's been lately?"

Danny stood frozen for a moment. That one hurt way more than he would ever let on.

"Truthfully," Danny raised his eyebrows and looked back into the horizon. "I guess I haven't *fully* recovered. Imagine having a puzzle that was seventy-five percent complete. The other twenty-five percent is sitting in a pile and has to be properly pieced together with the rest of the puzzle to get the full picture... That's how it is.

"It's all there, but some stuff is just a blur. I remember a lot of the really big stuff. Our first meeting. Most of my agency training. A lot of my martial arts training. But it's all the little things that made me the best, that gave me the edge... That's what's blurred. I guess a symptom of the injury."

Vanessa shook her head. Her concern for him was obvious by the way she looked at him.

"Your brain was never injured. Danny, your injuries are mental. Remember what the doctor said? You're repressing your memories as some form of subconscious protection. You have to let yourself remember."

"Vanessa..." Danny took a brief pause. "I haven't felt like myself since the injury."

Danny could remember most of his victims' screams from two decades of service. He could even remember some of their faces just before he pulled the trigger. Most had prayed to God for a miracle. God never answered their calls. Usually, there was that beginning of a scream, the sound of his gun firing, and then their body dropping. Why couldn't his brain repress those memories instead?

"Then you need to get yourself back into treatment," Vanessa said. "You need to start seeing somebody again."

"What if I don't want to ever remember?" Danny asked in a low tone.

"You're going to want to remember this!" A male voice called out from the foyer.

Vanessa turned first and rolled her eyes when she saw who was speaking.

"You have a key to this place?" she asked.

"Yes, as a matter of fact, I do," Peter Jacobs said with a large smile. His outfit was the opposite of Danny's. A muscle-tight shirt and jeans. His clothes showed off his buff figure.

Danny smiled big and hugged his friend tightly.

"Vanessa," Danny said. "Did you know that Peter and I have been friends since grade school? That's how long we go back!"

"So, you've both told me. A *million* times." Vanessa said as she extended her arms out for a hug. "It's good to see you, Peter. What brings you here? I thought you were on the road?"

Peter took a seat on a chair next to them and kicked his feet up. He pulled out his phone.

"Where's that big lug of a championship belt you were carrying around?" Danny asked.

"I lost the title. Thanks for knowin' Dragon Heart!"

Vanessa could not contain her smile. At least one other person still looked at him as Dragon Heart like she did. It was his martial arts alias. It was the nickname he had gotten in his early years in the Central Intelligence Agency fighting alongside Vincent Diezego.

"I thought you were going to be champion for a while?"

"Well," Peter shrugged. "I lost it on the last Monday night show, and now I'm on a break. My body's aching all over. Anybody who calls professional wrestling fake can fuck off. Because I can tell you, ain't anything fake about the pain that I feel."

Danny sat down next to Peter, "What brings you here unannounced, anyways?"

"Two parts. Number one, I've been genuinely worried about you. Whatever accident you got working for the State Department. It is the State Department you both work for, right?" He asked, narrowing his eyes.

Without hesitation, they both nodded yes.

"So... You got shot at on a diplomatic mission?" Peter squinted.

Danny nodded quickly.

"Yep, that's it."

Peter brushed him off with a laugh.

"Whatever the fuck you're into, brother, it's probably best I don't ask. Vanessa, when you going to run for the Senate? Show them how to get shit done?"

Vanessa smiled because she knew he was being sincere.

"That's not my path anymore. I'm content with my current plans."

"Well, I'm just thinkin' a profession that doesn't get you two shot at. But then again, with how fucked up this world is getting, I don't know what profession is safe from that anymore. You could come be a professional wrestler with me. Despite the physical toll, it's a family, and it's the most rewarding job on the damn planet. I've literally seen the world.

"I've been trying to get Danny to consider it since before you met him. Imagine the name, 'Dragon Heart' Danny Richmond, Heavyweight Champion of the World! You're both already two of the deadliest fighters on the planet, highly esteemed. The storyline writes itself!"

Peter laughed again. His laugh was contagious, as was his smile. There was an immediate levity brought to the situation.

"What's the second reason you're here?" Danny asked.

"I have some news for you," Peter slapped Danny's thigh, "The Golden Dragon Tournament."

Vanessa's smile faded. *Vincent Diezego. Xings. No. Please, no.* She knew immediately. Vanessa was also here for the Golden Dragon Tournament, but she had not intended to tell Danny that yet.

"It'll be the perfect way to get you back to your old self," Peter said, "Think about it! You've said a lot of times in the last year that the little things that made you the best are all a blur, right? How might the tournament help remedy that?"

Vanessa went to speak, but Danny beat her to it, "Could force me to get back to where I was. To find myself again. I won that tournament many times. I started calling myself Dragon Heart because of what that tournament meant to me."

"I don't like this," Vanessa said. Her concern for Danny was genuine.

"Do you like anything I've come up with lately?!" Peter said with a laugh. "I'm kidding. I promise. I'm kidding."

"No, honestly, I haven't," Vanessa didn't laugh.

"Think about it," Danny stood up and paced the balcony. "The best fighters from all around the world come to participate in this no-holds-barred tournament. The only rule is no killing your opponent. Every fighter with any prestige vies to get into this thing. To be its champion is a tremendous honor. To win means you're the best fighter on the planet."

Peter rose to his feet and walked around in his own excitement. Vanessa stood still, watching both of them feed off of each other's energy.

"Toxic masculinity at its finest..." she muttered.

"You're like the strict parents from a teen romance comedy, Vanessa," Peter said.

Vanessa massaged her temple.

"So, they're down for me coming back in then?"

"Yes, they are," Peter said.

"Excuse me?" Vanessa squinted, "I'm confused here. Danny, did you already accept?"

"I told Peter to let them know that if they do want me back in the tournament, then I accept the challenge. So, yea, I'm in," Danny said nonchalantly.

"What?!" Vanessa said. "Who-Who the fuck challenged you out of nowhere?!"

"Oh, just an old friend," Danny said without regard. "Anyways, Peter, you entering too?"

"Danny, why do you always do such irritational things?!" Vanessa threw her arms out with her eyes widened. Danny could feel her blood boiling.

"Please, calm—"

"Don't even try to tell me to calm down!" She cut Danny off. "Who challenged you?"

"Vanessa," he put his hands up. "I need this."

"Who challenged you?" She leaned in closer to him.

"Vincent..." he said.

Vanessa's eyes pressed shut for a moment.

"It's the best way," Peter stepped in. "Vincent Diezego's known Danny longer than anyone. They're childhood friends. Didn't Vincent work in the government with you for a while? I know you two went into the Marine Corps together."

"Peter, would you mind getting me a drink in the kitchen?" Vanessa asked with a big smile.

Peter nodded, "What do you want?"

"The usual."

"That kind of day, huh? Alright, alright." Peter immediately walked off.

Vanessa got close to Danny, and her smile faded.

"Peter may not understand what actually happened between you and Vincent, but I do!" Vanessa shouted in a whispering tone.

"I don't need to hear this right now." Danny brushed her off.

"But you do. This ain't the Marines or the CIA. He's not—"

"What flavor?" Peter asked while stepping back out onto the balcony.

"Watermelon," Vanessa said.

"Good pick. You know, you ever try bacon flavor Vodka? It's actually a thing!" Peter said.

Vanessa shook her head no and looked back to Danny.

"You should really try Bacon flavor," Peter continued. "I actually did, and it tasted fuckin' awesome. I was on a date with this really hot chick, and she liked it too. I mean, just the diversity of flavors."

Vanessa was tapping her foot and breathing heavily. Peter kept talking for another minute, with Vanessa grinding her teeth behind her forced smile.

"Peter, I'm actually really thirsty," Vanessa said.

Peter nodded and retreated back into the kitchen.

"I don't need you to tell me about our past, Vanessa. Do you know how many missions Vincent and I did together? We literally saved the fuckin' world together. He, Selena, and I. We were unstoppable. Vincent and I took bullets for each other. We were blood brothers..."

"*Were.* He's changed since then. The heroic soldier and operative you knew has been replaced by a monster. Do you get that?! You two haven't spoken in almost a decade! Remember what happened the last time you two fought in that tournament?!"

"Hey, do you just want the Vodka drink or perhaps some hard liquor too? You seemed pretty stressed," Peter observed, peeking his head out the door.

Vanessa remained silent, but Danny read the rage in her eyes.

"Peter, big daddy, I'm sure she'll be fine with just the Vodka." Danny said calmly.

"I'm going to try the hard liquor. I'm in that type of mood for some reason. Honestly, I'm really missing the business hardcore and whatnot."

Danny finally gave Peter a look that halted his speech. Peter threw his hands into the air, and he disappeared back into the kitchen.

"I remember what happened the last time. I don't even know how I made it out of that alive. That was when everything between us fell apart. I defeated him in the main event many times in a row, and then he went apeshit, and I blew it. He's never stopped being my brother, though. He has to be in there somewhere."

"This whole fucking thing is foolish," Vanessa said. "How about the Xings? How about the fucking hard drive we found that is now missing? You know, they're everywhere now. They're winning in Hungary, they've won in Venezuela, they've won in a certain number of countries in Northwest Africa. Their momentum needs to be stopped. We can do it. You want to find yourself again—"

"Sorry, one last question," Peter said. "What do you want, Danny?"

Vanessa rocked her fist in a struggle to stay calm.

"Just a glass of wine will do this time," Danny said.

Peter was gone again.

"If you want to find yourself again, then let's get you back into treatment and then back with me into the CIA as a consultant. I've been in touch with the agency about you."

"In touch with what agency?" Peter asked with drinks in hand.

"State Department," Danny said while taking his drink. "I'll be right back."

Vanessa took her drink, and before she could take a sip, Peter started.

"Okay, give me a chance to explain myself. I know Danny's not well, and I know Vincent is wild. I grew up with the motherfucker too! But Danny *needs* this. You told me before what the doctor said. What better way to kickstart his friggin' heart than bringing him back to his roots?"

"His roots?!" Vanessa pointed at Peter and then turned away to look out at the horizon. She set her drink on a table. Her main reason for keeping Danny out of the tournament was for his own protection. She did not want him to get hurt. The other was steeped in secrets she could never share with Peter. There were intelligence reports that a fighter in the tournament was carrying the hard drive that had gone missing. Those reports were enough for the agency to authorize her to investigate the tournament in any way she had to.

Danny walked back in with his drink gone.

"Vanessa," Danny said. "You believe in me, right?"

"Yes, of course, I do. But do you believe in you?"

"Yes," Danny said.

"Alright then. So, you're entering no matter what?" Vanessa said.

"Yes."

"Then I'm entering too."

"What?!" Danny's eyes widened, and his arms flew to his sides, "Excuse me?! Do you know what this tournament is?! Do you know how dangerous it is!"

"I think that is a bitchin' idea!" Peter shouted with glee.

"Shut it!" Danny pointed at Peter.

"Oh, what? Because I'm a woman I can't handle it?" Vanessa said, "Cut it with that patriarchal bullshit! Maybe you oughtta look in the mirror, asshole. A full-contact tournament where the only rule is no killing. It's no holds barred, and if people are going to be fighting, so will I."

"For what purpose?" Danny asked.

"A little bit to save your ass from Vincent and then mostly, to be crowned as the best damn fighter in the world." Vanessa crossed her arms with her eyes narrowed. She would keep the part about it being an official CIA mission to herself for now.

"Why? Do you plan to drop out now?" Vanessa asked.

"No, I don't," Danny said.

"Well, then, neither do I," Vanessa said.

Danny's heart was racing, and Vanessa's clearly was too. The tension between them was ready to explode.

"This is great!" Peter shouted in jubilee, "It's like putting the band back together! The three amigos. Entering the tournament to whoop some ass! Hey, help me with the punchline. A professional wrestler and two State Department employees walk into a bar..." He started laughing at his own joke.

Peter went back into the kitchen, already looking for another drink.

Vanessa stared off into the sunset, thankful to have another few seconds alone with Danny. She could hear Peter rustling around the kitchen, but her mind could not escape the last doctor's appointment with Danny just a month ago.

"Miss Rodes," The doctor's words were etched into her mind. "Physically, Danny is fine. He suffered zero brain damage. He barely has a dang scar on his head from the wound. Do you know what Post Traumatic Stress Disorder is?"

"Yes." She knew all too well but could never tell the doctor that.

"Danny's subconscious brain has decided to block out some of his memories as a way to protect him. It's all there. He just has to access it."

"But how? What can get him to that point of remembering?"

"He can bring it back piece by piece through heavy therapy, or I fear one day it may get triggered all at once from some sort of event. He needs help."

Vanessa escaped her own memory and came back to the present. She looked at Danny standing next to her. She was certain she saw tears fighting to escape his eyes.

"Why won't you let me in?" Vanessa asked.

"What the hell do you mean?" Danny said.

"This fuckin' mansion, these ridiculously expensive clothes, the gold watches. What the hell is all this?! What happened to your house in Chicago? What happened to the simple living?"

Danny said nothing, and she continued out of concern, "Danny, will you please just open up a little? Is this the life you really want to live? You were one of America's greatest heroes. I know you're traumatized, angry, and enraged about what happened, but you know as well as I do it's the job we were chosen for. We knew the risks going into it. You said that yourself earlier."

Vanessa paused only for a moment, "And now you want to just enter into this tournament? Blindly? Look, if you're scared to come back to the agency because of your memory issues, then I get that but then how the *fuck* do you justify entering into a no holds barred tournament with Vincent fuckin' Diezego?"

"Vanessa..." Danny tapped his fists against the railing. "You don't get it... When I got shot, your purpose was to see me through to recovery, right?"

"Of course."

"And then you went back to the agency and found another purpose there?"

"You're damn right. A lot of purpose."

"I haven't felt purpose since waking up." Danny's eyes began to water. "Every day has just been an empty void with no mission. When you went back, I got closer with Maryse. She showed me this new life. Even helped set me up with a real good job doing day trading at an office."

"And how is that job going?" Vanessa asked.

"I told my boss to go fuck himself yesterday and walked out." Danny held back the tears wanting to flow.

"Weren't you making really good money?"

"Yea. More money than ever… But it was without purpose. I sat in a cubicle all day, doing meaningless work making six figures. Every day was the same thing. Rinse, wash, repeat. And every single fuckin' day I got home, I felt even emptier on the inside. So, you see…

Danny stared into her eyes, "That's why I need this tournament. I need something to bring me back to life. I need a mission again. I'm desperate, Vanessa… You don't realize how hard it's been for me… When I look in the mirror, I don't recognize the soul staring back at me."

"Danny…" Vanessa whispered. "What's happening to you?"

"I don't know…" Danny whispered back. "I don't know…"

CHAPTER FOUR

The tattoos painted down his arm told the story of a soldier who had lived a thousand lifetimes. One stood out above all others. A dragon swirled around the letter R.

"Are you sure this is right, Raphael?" the woman asked. She was older than him but seemed healthier, less weathered than her male counterpart.

Raphael Johnson carried nothing. All he had were the clothes on his back. Raphael was from Bassakru, a country located in northern Africa on the west coast near the countries of Togo and Benin. The country had a rich history that, in recent times, had been tainted by fascist occupation.

The sounds of the sea crashed against the harbor. He could smell the salt water penetrate his nostrils while the ocean's breeze soothed him.

His Bassakran accent was thick, "Aunt Mary, there is nothing I am more certain of."

Raphael's body was petite but muscular and bore a plethora of permanent scars.

Mary noticed these immediately, and it worried her, "You don't look well."

Raphael stood against the harbor's railing, with the Statue of Liberty conquering his vision. He was in awe at its beauty and what it stood for. His eyes were glued to it, "I haven't felt well lately. Know what I mean?"

Mary ran her hand down his arm, "Ralph, stay here with me in America. No damn soldiers breathing down your neck."

"I hear there are no papers needed for travel?"

"For the most part." Mary said, smiling wide. "Only a driver's license, and that's if I am stopped. Which happens more than you might think. The conditions here are still better than back home, but there are problems."

"Do you ever admire this statue?"

"Of course. The architecture is beautiful. You see it enough times though and it becomes underwhelming."

"My brother and I talk about this in Bassakru," he said, the ocean's breeze seeming to cut through his clothes. "About the statue and what it means. My brother, he tells me about it all the time and even carries a picture of it with him. He was born and raised here, and so he has brought back stories of this place, this statue. I don't know if I believe him, but I trust him. His father is a warrior too. We taught each other how to fight and how to stand up to the Xings."

"How do you intend to stand up to them here? Raphael, please, listen to me. You have an out now. Sirleaf has been filling your head with that resistance talk, hasn't she?"

Raphael said nothing to her. He knew what he was fighting for and never regretted it.

"You are right," Mary said, leaning against the railing and taking in the image of lady liberty. "It is beautiful. Just please believe me, there is injustice everywhere. Even in America. And this cause you speak of? Is there no talking you out of it? No talking you to safety?"

"None. I won't stop till Bassakru is free. Have you heard of what they do to us?"

Mary's shoulders sunk into her chest, "Very little, it is barely talked about in the news, and politicians here do not dare speak of it. There is a silence in America to the struggle of our people, to the oppression. Lots of inaction, very few heroes. It's a very saddening sight."

Raphael turned around and leaned against the rail to observe the thousands of people walking among them. Some appeared angry, others were in a hurry, and some bore expressionless faces. Many of them, however, were plastered with the face of happiness. Parents walked with their kids across the coast and snapped pictures with lady liberty in the background. The sounds of pigeons could be heard over the low rumble of conversation and the rattle of laughter. All of these noises sounded unfamiliar to Raphael.

A little boy and girl ran across the guard rail together with their faces beaming. They laughed and shouted at each other.

The parents stood only ten feet away, recording them with their smartphones. The siblings ran around in circles with utter joy. They embodied the very innocence that could only come from children. For Raphael, their playtime moved in slow motion.

Raphael exhaled while his face remained as expressionless as a stone, "Do you hear the children playing?"

"Yes," Mary said, knowing what he was getting at, and it broke her heart.

"It's a world I never knew. By the time I was their age, the virus had begun to ravage our country, and then after that, the Xings took power."

Mary turned to him, "I know."

Raphael looked at her, "This country must know the true suffering of our people. They must know what the hell we've been through. The carnage, the darkness, and the tears. Do you know how many of my friends died before they could grow up?"

Raphael caught the eyes of another pack of kids on skateboards. They raced through the crowd of people angering some while garnering laughter from others. The juvenile antics were done with the confidence of immature teenagers who knew no real consequence would come.

Raphael watched another family stroll by. A mother pushed a baby stroller around while the father ran his hand down her back. They both took a moment to stare at each other with a twinkle in their eyes. What they had was true love that was free and unrestricted. Their eyes gave off vibrations of hope, progress, and an exciting future yet to come.

Raphael muttered, "They are so carefree."

Mary stared at the same family, "Certain people here, they are born into that optimism. It is a privilege they do not understand."

"The way the families move out in the open," he turned back around to stare at the statue, and she did too. "This is proof that the fascists can be beaten. Hope is here. We are standing in a world where it has been defeated. I cannot give up the fight in Bassakru."

"You have a lot to learn about the United States. I have to ask you again," Mary said, urgency creeping into her voice. "What is it that you plan to do here?"

"I am going to seek the help of a fellow freedom fighter. I was told many, many stories about him from my American brother. He has never met him personally but knows many who have. It is said that this man is known to fight fascists head-on and win. The resistance needs a man like him."

"What is his name?" Mary asked.

"Danny Kyle Richmond. He works for the United States government and has many resources. He has the connections to get aid to the resistance and, if we are lucky, join in the fight himself."

"So that is why you are here? To seek help from the American government?"

"I have something Danny Richmond will want," Raphael said. "You're better off not knowing what it is."

Raphael read the inscription on the Statue of Liberty's book, "Give me your tired, your poor, your huddled masses yearning to breathe free."

The words were inscribed into his very being and ran through his blood. He knew of the world he wanted to make for Bassakru and found the hope for it in America.

"We must get the Americans to help us. Danny Richmond has the resources."

"And how do you plan to reach him?"

Raphael turned to her, and the sun sparkled off of his eyes, "By entering the Golden Dragon Tournament."

Vanessa didn't need to rely on stories about the low-income neighborhoods of Chicago. She grew up in one. Now she stood in front of a one-story house in the center of one of the roughest. The fence surrounding the yard was rusted and tilted over. The lawn was made up of dead grass and random debris.

She rang the doorbell and observed the neighborhood around her. Bars covered windows and vehicles—some ravaged, some beautiful—filled driveways. She took note of the looks she got from every person who walked by. If only they knew she had been where they are.

The door opened to Vincent Diezego standing on the other side. His dark hair had a natural spike to it and made his face seem long and lean. His body had a classic V-shape. His muscles bulged from his shirt, and his dress pants gave him an elegant look.

"Damn," he said, smiling as his eyes took note of Vanessa's figure. "Vanessa Rodes, I take it? In the CIA and in the field, they regard you as the fastest gun in the west."

"Yes, I am she. May I come in?" She asked, ignoring his glance.

Vincent chuckled and waved his hand for her to step through.

Vanessa walked into the house. The walls were covered in unfinished paint jobs. The couches were littered with tears, and clothes were scattered everywhere. The signs of poverty were all too familiar for Vanessa. The echoes from her childhood followed her wherever she went. She never forgot duck-taping the holes in her shoes or her parents skipping meals for themselves so that she could eat.

"Sit down on any couch," Vincent said.

Vanessa sat down at the far end of a couch. Vincent sat down on the other couch. The table in between them gave her comfort and time to react. She was also closest to the exit. It was enough for her to ignore the smell of cigarette smoke.

He grabbed his cigarette from the ashtray and took a drag. "Care for a cigarette?"

"No thanks," she said.

"Well, speak. What caused the great Danny Richmond to send his squeeze to grace me with her presence, hm?"

"Firstly, Danny doesn't know I'm here. Secondly, I'm not his squeeze. We're best friends."

Vincent laughed, "What do you want?"

Vanessa sighed, "Solutions."

"Kid, sometimes everything turns to shit, and you can't change it. God's way of showing you he's there, I guess."

Another smell pierced her nostrils. *Green Apple?* The smell was more powerful than the cigarettes. She looked around at the house in disarray. The smell was relaxing and reminded her of the outdoors. *How the fuck can this house smell so good?*

"Vincent," she asked, forcing herself to say what she had to say. "Why are you challenging Danny again? Why do you two have to fight? You two were best friends, brot–"

"I know what we were, and the keyword there is *were*. Danny turned his back on me when I needed him most."

"That's blasphemy, and you know it. He–"

"He what? Kept true to the country? Listen, if you're here to talk me out of challenging him, you're wasting your damn time. I have a score to settle with that son of a bitch, and I'm going to settle it."

"So, you're just like him. Stubborn, short-sighted, and eager to crush the other one?"

Vincent shrugged his shoulders while chuckling, "If it makes me stubborn, then I guess, yea, I am."

"I have a deal for you..." Vanessa said.

"What kind of deal?"

"Not that asshole."

"Had to try..." Vincent shrugged.

"You informed about the rising Xing threat? The DLX?"

"I know enough. Why do you ask?"

Vanessa sighed in frustration, "I want Danny to come back, at least for a consultant role. It's imperative that he does." Vanessa leaned forward. "The 'Cold War' between U.S. Intelligence and the

Xings is growing much hotter than what is publicly known. The world is heading for a crisis."

"The fuck does any of this have to do with yours truly?" Vincent asked.

"Danny is obsessed with this idea that you two can repair what you had. That you're the key to his recovery."

"And what is it that you want?" Vincent asked. "Because I know damn well you didn't come here for him. I've heard a lot about you. You're one of the brightest in the intelligence community."

"Well," Vanessa sat upright. "I'm offering you a job. A chance to come back. Look, Danny is going through what he is. He has to heal in his good time. But the Xing threat will not wait for our best soldiers to recompose themselves. The country needs you, Vincent... Hell, you'll be well paid. How does that sound? You drop out of the tournament, and in exchange, you join the fight again?"

Vincent shook his head, "You got a lot of fuckin' nerve askin' me a question like that."

"Listen, I know what happened, and I under–"

"Do you? Did Danny really explain it? You think those fuckin' psychological evaluations really painted a picture of my mind? You read about me in some old, classified reports before you came here?"

"I read everything I could get my hands on. I got all the security clearances I needed."

"Figures." Vincent laughed for a moment. "Vanessa, you ever been hurt by the business yet? Have you lost things that you can't get back?"

Vanessa tried to hide the sudden anger, but her poker face broke just a little.

"Of course, I fuckin' have. Any operative who does the nature of the work we do has lost things. Regardless of my pain, I get my ass up and fight for this country every single day!"

"Then, as one officer to another, let me give you a piece of advice: Don't go back to the agency. Leave with your sanity while you still got it. Leave before they crush you because they will. It happens to everyone eventually."

"No, not always, and regardless, it's the job we were chosen for."

"Oh, Jesus Christ!" Vincent shouted with a chuckle while waving her away. "Of course, you'd say that! Of course! You still buy all that God and Country patriotic bullshit? That steady hand of propaganda they feed every operative?"

"Propaganda? No." She sat upright with more confidence than before. "I know damn well the injustices of my country. I had them forced upon me when I was born as a woman and had to be lectured as a teenager to walk with my keys in between my fingers. What I do, it's for the greater good. I got into this job to protect democracy. That's why I do what I do."

"I used to think like you, until the Iran mission."

"I read the reports on that."

"Fuck the reports. Let me correct your fuckin' understanding of what went down. Danny and I were on a mission, business as usual. We were deep in the center of Iran. It was supposed to be a simple snatch and run of files, but we got ambushed by 100s of Iranian soldiers in a twenty-story building. We called for backup, and they told us they couldn't send any. So, they left us there to die and we should have died. Instead, we killed enemy after enemy until we blew up half the building. We escaped with the files, leaving hundreds dead or burning alive.

"And when we got back... I went home, sat on my couch, and popped open a bottle of vodka, called up my then-wife, told her I loved her. And where did Danny go? Back to Langley and handed them the files. They stabbed us in the fuckin' back, and Danny chose them. He turned on me. He tried to rationalize his actions as for the greater good, classic Danny Richmond. He was given a medal, awards, and praised for coming back, while I was denied my pension all because I left the CIA before my contract was up, before the mission was officially complete.

"I got angry, told them I wanted my money, or I'd go public, so what did they do? They blacklisted me. They wiped out every cent I had in my account. I lost my beautiful house and wound up here, in this shithole. You know, had they come back for us, had they done the right thing, they may have been able to save what was left of my soul. Danny thinks it was the loss of the bullshit anti-psychotics that sent me over the edge, but it wasn't. It was that."

He sucked on his cigarette and blew more smoke, "They stole my sanity, my purity, my emotions, and my life on that night. And now," he raised his voice, "I'm known as a traitor to a country that betrayed me first!" his words transformed into a scream, "Well I am tired of helping the greater good when the people don't even give a damn about me!"

Vanessa replied, "Danny tried to help keep you on your feet."

"I know what he tried to do, and I don't care. He made it clear whose side he was on when he went back."

"No, he went back for the cause, not because he sided with the government. You must see that."

Vincent chuckled, "It doesn't really matter now, does it? The point of the story is... Vanessa, get out while you can. It took Danny a decade more to see it my way, but after his accident, he gets it. The government doesn't care about you. You know what's going to happen once you lose it like we did? They'll tell you to either go home or go on the next mission, and that's all they'll say. They won't care about how you feel. They care about their status quo, nothing more."

"You talk as if this is a secret to me," Vanessa said. She couldn't help but think of their response after Danny was shot. *No authorization granted.* In many ways, she agreed with Vincent, but she had a mission to accomplish.

Vanessa continued, "I know how the game works. Not everybody in government is a saint. I hold anger for what they did to Danny, but I refuse to forget right and wrong. My mission is to topple a fascist regime that's committing mass murder and spreading tyranny around the globe. We must protect democracy."

"Also," Vanessa said. "I'm calling you on some bullshit. Let's not act like you haven't still been active on the side, making money. And I'm not talking about the tournament."

"How you figure?"

"Oh, come on. Don't insult me like that. I know damn well the hitman jobs you've been up to the last eleven years. The agency knows too. You're a gun for hire. Your kill count didn't freeze once you left the agency."

"Touché. You have done your homework."

"I have. I refuse to let the sins of the past impact my judgment on what to do today."

"They'll take away your life one day, and your judgment won't mean a damn thing to you..."

"But forget all that for now," Vincent said, ogling Vanessa's body. "Why don't we just get to know each other personally?"

Vanessa's face crumbled in disgust, "Not in a million years, Vincent."

Vincent smirked, "Ah, I get it. Saving yourself for Danny. You're in love with him, aren't you?"

"That's none of your concern, and you know what? This is where I leave."

Vanessa stood up to leave and was met by Vincent doing the same, "Wait, hah, I'm serious. You're in love with him. Does he even see it?"

"No..." she looked to the ground. "He doesn't."

Vincent laughed louder than before, "Hah, you and Danny are a lot alike. Both of you are clueless to the fuckin' world around ya. Why do you wait for him?"

"I don't wait for him. What I do is my business only."

"Indulge me," Vincent said.

Vanessa shrugged, "Nah, I'm good."

Vincent continued, "Funny, I wonder how long you two have had feelings for each other but were too occupied with the mission to see it."

Vincent started to laugh, "You know Danny, he's never had a relationship that's worked. His lifestyle prevents it. Damn boy's always been wild, hell I remember one time just before he and I went to our mission in 1990, we brought this woman home from a club, and we both tag tea–"

"Don't even finish that damn story. I'm out of here."

Vanessa charged past him to the door.

"Hold on, hold on. Why wait around for that idiot Danny? You could just have a good time with me."

Vanessa spun to look at him and observed the horrendous conditions around the house. She stopped to stare at him, "Not if it meant my life. Now, why don't you clean up this shithole? You being in this position now is nothing more than your own pathetic self-pity."

Vanessa opened the door and began to walk out as Vincent said, "I'd be careful in this part of town. Don't stop at the red lights."

"Thanks for the heads up. By the way... I'm entering the tournament, and I plan to win the whole fuckin' thing, so watch yourself."

Vincent let out a boisterous laugh as he plopped onto the couch and grabbed the bottle of Vodka. Vanessa slammed the door shut and made her way to the car with her mind on the world. She was startled to see the fury in Vincent's eyes, something dark was brewing inside of him, and she could feel it.

Hours later, Vanessa found herself sitting against the wall of a balcony attached to her apartment in Chicago. She could see the city skyline from her window with her laptop on the table next to her. Her meeting with Vincent was fresh on her mind while she read through an intelligence report sent to her on an encrypted server.

```
Classified: Destroy After Reading
From: Puerto, R.
```

Subject: Memo on Lost Item and Person of Interest.

Mission Update:

Name of suspect is Raphael Johnson, leader of the Bassakran Resistance. He is known for inciting violent uprisings against Xing governments. He is in his mid-twenties. The hard drive whereabouts were last reported falling into Bassakran Resistance hands. He is believed to have arrived in the United States today with the hard drive. His motivations are currently unclear to us. Parallel intelligence reports with supplemental information from other agencies gathers Xings are also in town looking for this hard drive.

Orders:

Track the Suspect and monitor his actions in this tournament. Physical Force and interception are not yet authorized. Decipher his motivations and only intercept if there are attempts from the suspect to sell or give the hard drive to others. Figure out if the suspect is a friend or foe. Be on the lookout for Xings, who may be coming after him and are present at the tournament. Deadly force is only authorized in self-defense situations. Enter the tournament as planned and go as deep as you need to. Continue your efforts to recruit former operatives to your cause.

End Message.

Vanessa looked at a photo of Raphael included in the report. She committed his face to memory before deleting the message entirely. Vanessa knew this mission was touchy. Her job in the CIA was primarily done on foreign soil. The Federal Bureau of Investigations typically handled domestic threats like this, but because of the importance of this hard drive to the agency, Raphael being a foreigner, and the potential for the Xings to be foreigners, it allowed the CIA the authority to conduct a mission on home soil. So long as she stayed in her lane, that is. Vanessa was certain her reports were probably going to be shared with FBI agents in the event any threats had to be arrested.

Vanessa made quick work typing her updated report to her superior. She updated them on the status of Danny Richmond and Vincent Diezego. She wrote her report in a way that protected Danny from any more aggravation from CIA upper management. She would focus on bringing him back in when it was safe for him and he was healthy to do so. If that time never came then, she was not going to put his life at risk. No matter her mission, she would never go back on the pact she made with her best friend.

Vanessa sent her report and safely closed out all encrypted systems. She switched screens and opened up her own personal journal document. She stared off into the city skyline while connecting with her own emotions. She started to type away.

From the personal journal of Vanessa Rodes:

It's May. I am not sure how to start this other than to say that I am worried. Primal rage, that's what was in Vincent's eyes as I spoke to him. He wants to crush Danny, not just for the sport of being the best, but to satisfy revenge that has built up in him for over a decade. I have seen rage like his, and it is usually from terrorists we have tracked down. And yet, I remember my parents choosing between gas money and food. Now that I look back on it, my parents used to forgo their own healthcare and food so they could provide both for me. So, in some ways, I understand his rage. Vincent grew up in hell too, different than mine, but still hell. It follows me wherever I go. In whatever I do. It does the same to Vincent. My run-in with Vincent has me reflecting on my own childhood. I'll never forget how badly medical debt and hospital bills had crushed my parents financially.

Beyond all that, I still can't escape my guilt about Danny. I so often wonder what life would look like if I had just acted a second faster and shot that Xing before he tackled me in the jungle. Danny wouldn't have been shot trying to recover the hard drive I lost. I can't shake that guilt. The accident sent his life in a downward spiral. I nearly got him killed. How does one make peace with that? Vincent wants to crush him. How can I just do nothing? The agency put me on a mission to enter the tournament. Danny entering complicated matters but gave me a secondary mission, protecting him like I failed to before.

Funny, really, Danny and Vincent are wasting time going to war with each other while the world burns. Danny, Vincent, and I could crush the Xings, and yet, here we are instead, crushing each other.

CHAPTER FIVE

Everything about her sang extravagance. Her tanned skin seemed to be without flaws. Her silky brunette hair ran down to her back. Her face was covered with makeup that only accentuated her glow. She was the center of attention in the photo shoot. The studio's lighting was constructed to compliment her complexion. The four-cornered room was filled with photographers, video cameras, lighting technicians, and beauticians.

Maryse Antoinette flipped through her modeling portfolio while speaking to her agent in French. Studio hands deconstructed the set piece by piece.

"Take this," Maryse said. "This is what I want you to show them. Tell them the price I require for the next shoot, and when they offer it, you may accept on my behalf. Book it for at least a few weeks out, understood?"

"Yes, ma'am." Her agent nodded, and then he walked away with her portfolio in hand.

The price of Maryse's outfit and jewelry were excessive, yet their elegance made up for the cost.

Maryse walked over to a bench on one side of the room, where Danny Richmond stood up to greet her. They shared a passionate kiss and a tight hug.

"You looked wonderful today," Danny said.

Danny looked up and down at her. Nearly everything about her was perfect. Her accent was proof she was born and raised in Paris, France. Her family owned and operated a worldwide modeling empire.

She responded in another soft line of French, and Danny leaned in closer to her. His French had become rustier the longer he was out of active duty, but it still melted him when she spoke.

"It's been intriguing being a part of this world with you. It's so different than what I'm used to." Danny said. This entire world was foreign to him. Most people seemed to agonize over getting the correct lighting as if they were operatives hunting down a dangerous enemy. The world's troubles did not exist in this room. Maryse's problems were the only problems anyone seemed to care about.

"Is it not so much better than your world of war? My Daniel, while you are with me, I want you away from that horrible lifestyle."

Danny wondered how much he should have told her about Vanessa's visit. He decided to keep it quiet. To his disadvantage, Maryse seemed to notice his conflict.

"It is not as if you have to drink the sea." Maryse rolled her eyes. "I am simply telling you to stay away from that agency. Stay away from the guns. Live a normal life. Now, what happened to the job you were working? You were making good money, no?"

"You know what happened," Danny said.

"Oh, Daniel." She went off in French and then slid back into English. "This tournament you are going into will be good for you. You will get through it with ease and then return to the office. You had a lapse in judgment. It can be forgiven. The night brings advice."

He squinted, and she said, "It's a French saying that means to sleep on it."

Another voice chimed in, "I've heard that before." Vanessa Rodes said. "My favorite French quote comes from World War II leader Charles de Gaulle. Silence is the ultimate weapon of power."

"Hi, I'm Vanessa Rodes. Danny's talked a lot about you. It's nice to meet you." Vanessa stuck out her hand.

"Hmm. You are Miss Rodes. Nice to meet you." Maryse narrowed her eyes and looked the other way. She walked over to a table containing her makeup kit and a portable mirror.

"Why did you ask me here, Danny?" Vanessa asked and ignored Maryse.

Danny realized Maryse was still far enough away, "I'm gettin' a bit stir crazy in this place, and I know you wanted to talk more anyways."

"Yea, we're both out of our element here," Vanessa said.

Danny and Vanessa watched staffers push a rack with luxurious clothing Maryse had worn for the shoot. They nearly crashed into a table of makeup equipment. Danny and Vanessa both got a chuckle out of it.

"You're dead set on entering the tournament?" Vanessa said.

"Oddly, I really thought you wanted to talk just to catch up," Danny said.

They both laughed again.

"And they always call me the crazy one," Vanessa said. "I went to Vincent's house."

"You did what?!" Danny's eyes widened. How could Vanessa go there? Didn't she understand how dangerous it was?

"Why the fuck would you do something like that without telling me first?!"

"Oh, like I need your fuckin' permission to do anything? Cut it with that patriarchal bullshit. I can take care of myself. I grew up not far from there anyways. I tried to see if I could talk some sense into him." Vanessa said.

"Let me guess, he told you to fuck off?" Danny relaxed himself with no other choice.

"That he did. He even refused my offer to come back to the agency."

Danny laughed, "The seventh floor must really be desperate if they're authorizing his comeback too."

Vanessa shook her head and clearly ignored his slight, "Vincent plans to crush you. He's determined to hurt you.

"My Daniel is a superior fighter," Maryse said while latching onto his arm. "I do not share your skepticism in his abilities, Miss Rodes."

"Oh Jesus, he's got you buying into this too?" Vanessa said.

"I did not need to buy anything," Maryse said. "I simply believe in his ability to do the things he says he can. Perhaps you lack the strength to compete with this Victor character, but Daniel does not."

"It's Vincent," Danny said.

"Whatever." Maryse shrugged.

"My lack of strength?" Vanessa stared Maryse in the eyes. She kept her poker face strong without feeling the need to justify herself.

Danny knew Vanessa well enough to know when she was in fight mode. He also knew how quickly Maryse would be on the ground if she tried to engage Vanessa. He immediately stood in between both of them.

"How's about we all get something to eat?" Danny said.

"You and I can go together," Maryse said while staring at Vanessa.

Vanessa rolled her eyes, "I'm not dealing with this mean girl bullshit. Maryse, I don't know you. I have no beef with you. All I'm asking is that you help me talk this man out of his suicide mission."

"Explain to me how that is any different than the suicide lifestyle you want him to return to?" Maryse said.

"The hell you talkin' about?" Vanessa said and then looked to Danny. "Did you tell her your past?"

Danny took a step back.

"I know about his past life as an operative," Maryse smirked. "I plan on keeping him away from that."

"Jesus Christ!" Vanessa said. "So much for secrets."

"Perhaps," Maryse shrugged, "You will need God to save you, as I am confident Daniel will do fine in the tournament. You, however?"

Danny looked at Maryse with anger. Nobody talks to Vanessa like that. He took a step back and shrugged.

Vanessa stepped nearly nose to nose with Maryse. Vanessa's fists were balled up at her sides, "Listen to me. I don't know who you are or who you think you are. Maybe you're the negative influence pulling him astray or maybe you're just oblivious to the situation. What I do know is you've said the last rotten thing to me you're going to say tonight. We clear on that?"

Maryse took a step backward, and her eyes widened. Her shoulders seemed to sink into her chest.

Vanessa turned to Danny, "I'm entering the tournament, and I plan on getting to Vincent before you do. I'm going to prove I'm the best damn fighter in the world. Tomorrow, you meet with Peter and me, and we start preparing."

"Wait, what do you mean you're getting to Vincent before I can?" Danny said with his arms out. Vanessa was already making her way through the exit.

Danny bit his lip. He knew what lengths Vanessa would go to in order to accomplish her mission. He knew Vanessa could take care of herself and also knew how dangerous Vincent could be. Why would he be fighting Vincent then if he knew the risks? He couldn't fully answer that question himself. He just knew that he had to. He also knew how angry it made him that Vanessa would act as reckless as he was acting. How would he react if he knew she was hunting down Xings in the tournament too?

"Relax," Maryse said. "She is far too uptight. Probably jealous of your ability."

Danny turned to Maryse without a smile, "Don't treat Vanessa Rodes like that in my presence. She saved my life." His anger was visible and caused Maryse to step back again. It was clear she had not expected backlash.

Danny's phone began to ring. He pulled it out and saw his mom on the caller identification. He rolled his eyes and slipped the phone back into his pocket, totally unprepared to talk to the actual caller.

"Who was that? Vanessa?" Maryse asked.

"No. It was nobody." Danny wished it was Vanessa.

"I apologize. She's fragile, but what am I supposed to do?" Maryse grabbed Danny's hands. "She is clearly unhinged. Perhaps putting Vincent in his place will bring Vanessa to her senses. Now let's go eat."

"Yea. Food sounds nice," Danny said while staring off at nothing. His mind was yet again on Vanessa, Vincent, and the tournament. He felt like a runaway train about to fly off the tracks. He didn't know what his destination was or how he would traverse the journey ahead. All he knew was that he had to keep going. He had to stand up to his fears and stand up to himself.

It was nighttime. Vanessa was sitting in her parked vehicle in front of a restaurant. The car's exhaust billowed out through the pouring rain. The lights of the Chicago skyscrapers glazed across her soaked vehicle. She had the heat turned on full blast, and it brushed against her body. She looked back and forth, catching the eye of somebody walking toward her vehicle.

She popped the locks, and the person opened her passenger door, sitting down. He closed the door, and she hit the locks. He held a beige envelope in one hand and a paper bag in the other.

"Robert," Vanessa said with a nod and a smile.

Robert handed her the envelope. She popped open the top and looked inside.

"A decoy?" Vanessa asked.

"Yes," Robert said. "If Raphael is not a friendly, we may need to track him, and that has a GPS tracker installed. You swap out those hard drives. How you doing?"

Robert Puerto was only five foot three inches tall. He was a head analyst with the Central Intelligence Agency. What he lacked in field experience, he made up for with charismatic optimism, a charming personality, and an uncanny level of intellect. He was also loyal to the max and had become one of Vanessa's closest confidants.

"Pumped," Vanessa said. "I'm not gonna bullshit you, I'm a little excited to be in this tournament regardless of the mission. I do plan to actually win."

Robert ran his hand through his hair. He opened up the bag and handed her a sealed pasta dish along with utensils. He pulled out his own dish.

"From your favorite Italian Restaurant," Robert said.

"Fucking awesome!" Vanessa smiled. "Our drinks are in the cup holders."

They began to eat away at their meals at a brisk pace. Vanessa spent so much time away from home that she would often forget how good Chicago food was.

"You're braver than I am, fighting in this thing," Robert said. "The agency is a little worried that your desire to protect Danny will impede your judgment."

"They're not wrong," she said. "But what the fuck am I supposed to do? He pretty much took a bullet for me. I can't just leave him behind. I'm confused. Do they want Danny back or not?"

"They have you. That's all they need. They'll take Danny, hell even Vincent if they can, but they're not interested in spending too many resources on their recruitment." Robert said.

"Fuck that. Just speak the truth." Vanessa said. "They look at Vincent and Danny as baggage. Yet, we all know they have sources we don't have. They both command a certain level of respect on the field. Have you read the reports on Vincent's activities? His private hitman jobs have not been small targets. Some of his kills have been people we've been trying to take out for some time."

"I read that. Vincent's been busy since he left the agency. Upper management was content to let him do what they see as our dirty work. Probably why they've never stepped in."

Vanessa placed the decoy in her coat pocket and tossed the envelope in the back seat.

Vanessa continued on, "Vincent's not past his prime. He's deadlier than ever. Danny, once he gets his head on straight, will be a force too. Anyways, what am I looking for in this tournament? Give me the blunt assessment."

Robert wiped rain off his sleeve, "Keep an eye on Raphael. Watch his movements in between fights. We doubt you'll be able to identify any Xings during the tournament. They'll likely wait till Raphael makes his move. If you want to find the Xings, you'll have to track Raphael. Remember, you're not law enforcement. The seventh floor at Langley is uncomfortable with our operatives doing too much fieldwork on home soil. That means do this one by the book. So, no lethal force unless it's in self-defense. You come across somebody worth arresting, contact your FBI liaison. And another thing."

"Yea?" She looked at him.

"Are you sure you're good to do this mission? You know it's not your fault, right?" Robert said. He was referring to the day of Danny's accident.

"Easy for you to say. You didn't make the mistake that caused him to get a bullet to the head." Vanessa gulped. "I owe this to him, to fight Vincent first. I put him in that wheelchair."

"That's bullshit. You didn't put him in that chair. He doesn't believe that, and you shouldn't either." Robert said fiercely.

Vanessa shrugged, "I feel how I feel about it."

"Well then, I hope you win." He genuinely smiled. "You deserve this championship. Just don't be foolish out there. You ain't got nothin' to prove to anyone. I'm gonna stay in town and watch the tournament myself, I think. For intelligence purposes, of course."

"Despite my motivations, I am excited to be in this. The honor of being the best is something to aim for." Vanessa said.

"Does Danny know you're in this thing on orders?" Robert said.

Vanessa placed the lid back on her meal. She was going to save the best parts for tomorrow so that she could savor the taste.

"I told him about the part of me entering to protect him and to win it all," Vanessa said, "Which is the truth. I haven't told him about the mission. I'm worried it could make him a target if he knows, so for now, it's just me."

"Understood. What else do you need from me?" Robert said.

"Keep upper management off my back while I work this out. Keep feeding me whatever intelligence you're getting."

"I got you, sister."

Vanessa and Robert bumped fists. They continued drinking coffee and chatting about world issues involving the Xings. They discussed the Xing dominance in so many countries and its continued spread. They played out their dream scenarios of actions that the U.S. Government could take to bring the Xings to their knees. They realized their strategies were often in the minority opinion. They moved on to the tournament and the slate of fighters involved. Between getting Danny back to health, possibly recruiting Vincent, retrieving the hard drive, and finding a way to curtail Xing expansion, they knew they had an uphill battle ahead of them. Vanessa was going to have to swim through a sea of sharks and somehow make it to shore without a scratch.

CHAPTER SIX

Danny stood in his basement in front of a body-sized mirror, wearing workout clothes. His legs were well-conditioned and defined. A punching bag and other workout equipment was scattered throughout the basement. Soon Peter and Vanessa would be over, and some pre-tournament sparring would commence.

He wanted to be excited, but instead, he could only reflect on a year ago. He let his mind wander back to just weeks after he awoke from his coma.

Danny sat in his wheelchair with his hands to his face inside the physical therapy room. In front of him were two rails that stretched across the room at arm's width from each other. There was other rehabilitation equipment scattered throughout. Danny had to find a way to walk across it.

Tears had soaked his shirt, and his pride was in shambles. A physical therapist named Mark stood near him, calm and patient as Danny worked to contain himself. Danny was at the lowest point in his life, and he questioned his own value as a human being. He was a martial artist, a CIA Operative, and a Marine. Now all of that felt like a life he would never have again. For some reason, he could not escape this crazy idea that Vincent would come to his aid after being told about his accident. That day was never going to come.

Danny pressed his toes into the ground to make sure he still could. He ran his finger across his thigh to check the feelings in his leg.

"Where's Vanessa?" Danny asked.

"She stepped out to get something. Come on, Danny, you need to be able to do this." Mark said.

"I know. I'm just so fuckin' scared."

Danny closed his eyes and thought of his father's words. He took the deepest breath he had ever taken before to inhale his courage and exhale his fear. He remembered more of his training.

"You can do this one more time today," Mark said.

Danny opened his eyes, ready to take the next step.

His mind transported him to two months after that. Danny was taking his first steps without the assistance of a walker or guard rails. He focused on his toes and his legs, taking one step at a time near a field of grass. Vanessa stood twenty feet away from him with a warrior's glance. She was his biggest supporter and challenged him in every healthy way possible.

Danny carefully put one foot in front of the other. He limped, and his body tilted with each step. His legs were in pain with each step he took. The simple act of walking again came with the intensity of running a marathon. Eventually, Danny made it to Vanessa, nearly falling into her arms. Her words of encouragement fueling him along the way.

Confidence started to seep through. He did it. He took twenty steps without the assistance of anything. It hurt, and he nearly fell on his rear end, but he made an accomplishment. Walking again had become his new mission. It became his obsession that he would not back down from. He was a warrior, and he planned to overcome this obstacle just like he had every other one.

In the present, Danny moved away from the mirror to the punching bag. He was warmed up and ready to go. He took every footstep with an appreciation that only a journey like his could bring. Danny got into his fighting stance and thought about his rehabilitation. He thought about every ounce of blood, sweat, and tears it took for him to be able to do this again.

Danny rocketed his leg out for a roundhouse kick at warp speed. His shin smacked into the punching bag that swung back and forth on impact. Danny followed it up with the same kick from the other leg. He paused and took a deep breath to wrestle his emotions. He could not explain the sheer amount of pride and excitement that came with his kicks. Not too long ago, they seemed unthinkable. He waited for the pain that would force him to back out of the tournament.

He went for another roundhouse kick to the punching bag. He realized the pain wasn't coming because his legs were long since at 100 percent.

The bag afforded him the time to reflect after each strike. In the tournament, his opponents would not grant him that luxury. That blanketed his positive emotions with anxiety. He knew he could not back away from Vincent anyways. Danny had to stand up to his own demons. He had to know if he could still fight.

CHAPTER SEVEN

Danny circled in place to absorb every aspect of the amphitheater. The room's smell was as familiar as ever. The smell of decades of blood, sweat, and tears mixed in with the odor of a lemon-scented cleaner was prominent. The smell triggered a previously repressed memory. He remembered the first time he ever took in the amphitheater. The place had not changed much since then.

There was a digital read-out board to the north of the room. There were brackets for the thirty-two fighters, match times, and match outcomes. Underneath it, there was a long table enshrined with golden silk sheets for the top spectators that usually consisted of legendary fighters from the past. There were three statues of dragons set up behind the table.

In the west corner of the room was a set of tiered bleachers for the fighters to all sit in. On every side of the room, there was traditional stadium seating for all of the fans. The setup reminded Danny of a roman coliseum with the twenty-four by twenty-four-foot platform in the center of the room and the spectator seating engulfing them in a circle. Danny walked up to the platform. It was four feet in height. It was just as he remembered it.

When he had taken it all in, he made eye contact with Georgio Moroder, the promoter and owner of the tournament. His brown suit was more expensive than most monthly salaries. His hair was puffy, slick, and combed back. He had a lit cigar in his hand.

"Mr. Richmond, as you can see, not much has changed since you were last here," Moroder said. English was his second language, and though he spoke with a thick Italian accent, his English was perfect. "It's so good to see you again. It's been such a long time."

Nearly every fighter set to enter the tournament was in the amphitheater going through their paperwork, conversing, and soaking in the environment. The tension in the room was as thick as concrete. Each fighter made eye contact with the other as they walked by. All of them were sizing up their opponents. Some walked with forced dominance, while others were calm and collected. Every fighter was certain they would be the one victorious and everyone else the future loser.

"It is just as I remember it," Danny said to Georgio. "So many memories. I am amazed you've kept it the same."

"Mr. Richmond," Georgio replied. "The council and I have discussed it, and we believe it is imperative to keep the layout simple. A tournament with such honor does not need to be distracted with news cameras and fancy lights. The audience attending this tournament are exclusive, and with that exclusiveness comes respectful behavior and lots of money from our fans. Just a little over a thousand can be housed in this small arena. We will need every available seat with you and Vanessa entering the tournament."

Danny said, "Word got out quick, I imagine."

Georgio patted him on the shoulder, "Oh yes, really quickly. You are a high-priced commodity. The amount of money we're expecting to make for this tournament is more than the last two years combined due to the high-stakes betting going on now. We try to keep this tournament as underground as possible, but this year there will be no stopping the footage from going across the internet."

Danny asked, "More than the last two years combined? How's the turnout been?"

Georgio shrugged, "Turn out has been okay. The matches are all entertaining and very suspenseful, that is, until the main event. Vincent pretty much dominates any opponent he comes across. Rarely do the main event matches go over five minutes. His mere presence throws even the best fighters off their game. For the first time in a while, Vincent's victory is in question. Vanessa's the wild card. Her recognition is growing quickly, and let's just say some of us other high rollers have found a new pick to bet on winning it all. Once the people see her in action, I imagine she will become a fan favorite."

Vanessa Rodes leaned against the platform and made mental notes of all the fighters around her. She was sizing up her competition as well as looking for anyone who looked like they could be involved with the Xings. She paid attention to how they moved, their composure, and any visible soft spots on their body. Observing their body language, she could see who carried themselves with confidence and who carried themselves with cockiness. She could tell some came here for the sole purpose of dominating and others came here out of a respect for combat.

A fighter from Central America that stood a monstrous six foot six inches tall stopped in front of her. He ogled her body with his eyes moving from her breasts to her thighs. He stood there for an awkward half minute. She responded by making direct eye contact with him.

He twirled his head around, "Hey there, I'm Julian. Maybe you'd like to train together sometime?"

"No thanks," she replied and looked away.

"Oh, come on, smile! I'm just trying to be nice." He waited for her to respond, and when she did not, he shrugged. "You're not worth my time anyways. I doubt you'd last a second out there, pretty woman. Maybe you'd be best back at a hair salon or cashiering."

He continued staring for another few seconds. She stared at him again, and he finally walked away without acknowledging the awkwardness he had created without a care.

She mouthed, "I hope I get a chance to knock you out…"

Maryse interrupted her focused aggression, "Miss Rodes, are you sure you could take on a fighter like that?"

Vanessa kept her emotions hidden and responded plainly to Maryse.

"Do you even really care?"

Maryse swiped her thumb across her phone and scrolled through social media. She did not bother to make eye contact with Vanessa, "I really do not. I am not sure why I am even here."

"You don't get what this tournament represents to people like Danny and me," Vanessa said, like it was an accusation. "To all the fighters in this room."

Maryse kept her eyes locked on her phone. She stuck her phone out in front of her and puckered her lips to center the camera lens for a selfie.

"Whatever, ignore me. If you actually gave a damn about Danny, then maybe you'd care to know what's driving your man on a fuckin' suicide mission."

Maryse sighed loudly while placing her phone away, "Excuse me? You think I do not care about Daniel? You have not the slightest clue as to who I am. Just because I have fame and modeling, you think I am some sort of apathetic bimbo?"

Vanessa shrugged, "The thought had occurred to me."

Maryse shot back, "You are dead wrong. Tell me, what is this barbaric tournament? Why is the Gold Dragon so impactful to people like you? Why should I be worried about my man who has a history of glorious martial arts?"

"The Golden Dragon Tournament brings about the best fighters from all over the world," Vanessa said. "It is a full contact sport; the only rule is no killing. Your opponent could have broken bones, and if they do not submit and can still compete, the match continues. The three ways to win are by knock out, submission, or knocking your opponent off the platform. Fighters train their whole lives for this tournament.

"You won't see it broadcast on some cable news network because they are not allowed here. Video footage of these tournaments do leak out onto the internet now. It started out in America decades and decades ago, originally as a descendant of another legendary tournament out of Hong Kong. A Chinese fighter from that tournament was so impressed by the vigor, heart, and sheer brutality of the tournament that he wanted America to have its own version of it. So, he connected with Georgio Moroder, who was a known boxing and wrestling promoter here in the States. The sensei of the tournament, Yoshi Toroko. was brought along to give it real prestige. He is a former winner of many full-contact tournaments and, in his day, was known as one of the greatest fighters in the world. This tournament is known for sending many fighters to the hospital win, lose, or draw."

Maryse squinted, "So a bunch of men beat each other senseless for a small amount of honor. To call themselves the best fighter?"

Vanessa chuckled. She couldn't deny the truth in that statement, "Yes and no. It's more than just beating each other senseless. These fights, most of them are about respecting the art of your craft and presenting it to the world. A man well-versed in Brazilian Jiu-Jitsu from France may battle a man well-versed in Kung Fu from Argentina. There's no cash prize for the victor. There's the honor of knowing you've proven yourself to be the best. This tournament is the place where fighters can immortalize their legacy and show their mentors and loved ones that they honor them. Hundreds of fighters try to get into this tournament every year, but only thirty-two actually qualify." *My field combat history got me in.*

"Interesting. How did this tournament come to be called the Gold Dragon?"

Vanessa bit her lip, "Golden Dragon Tournament. In Chinese culture, golden dragons are associated with powerful deities or harvest. Golden dragons always symbolize wealth, prosperity, strength, harvest, and power. Being that the founder of this tournament is Chinese, he brought that here with him. Danny took on the alias 'Dragon Heart' from his time here in the tournament."

Vanessa noticed Maryse had her eyes locked into her phone once more, "Have I already lost you?"

"I heard all of what you said. My opinion of this has not changed, nor has my faith in Daniel to succeed."

Vanessa laughed, "Right. You didn't see him sparring with me. I got hits on him I should have never been able to get. He may weight lift, but he has not properly trained in some time, and he's holding back. He's walking into this fight with one arm tied behind his back and the other bruised. He can still get by, but not like before. Dragon Heart needs to return."

Vanessa took a deep breath and began to survey the room again. Convincing Maryse was a fool's errand. She took notice of a man in a tank top and fresh jeans. She noted the plethora of scars all over his body. The Dragon R tattoo on his arm confirmed she had found him. Raphael Johnson turned his head, making direct eye contact with her. They shared a powerful warrior's glance. In that moment, Vanessa could feel all of his pain and his sorrow. All of his determination and fears. It was written all over him. He did not work to hide any of it. Vanessa was ordered to decipher his motivations. She would need more time to complete that objective, but off the bat, she knew he was carrying the weight of his entire country on his shoulders.

Raphael and Vanessa shared an innate understanding of each other that came with their warrior's stare of respect. The difference between them is that she knew who Raphael was. It was clear Raphael did not know who she was. They kept eye contact a little longer for what felt like an eternity for both. Raphael's demeanor was different than everyone else. It was calm and respectful. He broke the contact with a polite nod and then walked away to hand in his papers to the event administrators.

She looked around for any other characters that stood out as potential Xing. *No one yet.*

On the other end of the room, Danny now stood by himself, staring at the empty platform. His mind sucked him back into his last battle with Vincent. The pain, the screams, and the terror became real all over again.

Vincent's crazed aggression struck fear in Danny as Vincent swung with a left hook. Danny leaned back, dodging the punch, and shot his heel into the air, aiming for Vincent's chin. Vincent sliced his hand through the air, chopping it into Danny's shin. Danny's bone screamed in agony as his body bent forward. Vincent spun around with his left fist in front of him. He came full circle and rocketed his knuckles into Danny's forehead. The blood already covering his face splattered as his head snapped back and forth.

Danny's own anxiety forced him back into the present. Against his will, he remembered the physical pain from that fight and the time it took to heal. His mind was on the verge of unlocking more, but he forced himself into another conversation with Georgio.

Another few hours went by, and the amphitheater was almost entirely empty.

Danny and Maryse were headed for the exit.

"You comin'?" Danny asked.

"Give me a few minutes," Vanessa said.

Danny and Maryse walked out the door while Vanessa walked across the empty amphitheater. She walked around the twenty-four-by-twenty-four platform. Its surface still wore the stains of blood, sweat, and tears from decades of fighters. Vanessa started plotting out her fight with Vincent in her head. And how she would make reality out of what was supposed to be impossible.

"Preparing yourself?" Georgio asked with his suit jacket hanging over his shoulder. He had another lit cigar in his hand. Georgio was beaming with confidence and presence as he always was.

"I wanted to pick your promoter brain." Vanessa leaned against the platform.

"Care for a smoke?" Georgio puffed on his cigar.

Vanessa shrugged, "Cuban?"

"Mhm."

In less than a minute, Vanessa had her own lit cigar. The smoke from both billowed in the air around them,

"Tell me, Georgio," Vanessa said. "What are the bets looking like right now?

Georgio rocked his fist in the air, unable to contain his excitement. He let the flavor of his cigar soothe him.

"Oh, it's crazy. I haven't seen anything like it in nearly a decade. Two mega powers are colliding at once. Danny Richmond's return and the possibility of another Danny-Vincent fight. And the other is, well, to be blunt, you."

"Go on." Vanessa nodded.

"Only one other woman has ever entered this tournament before, and she lost in the first round. You though, let's just say you've got people turning heads. Some of our clientele here really enjoy betting against the odds. Clientele have walked away with small fortunes doin' that. It's a common practice ya'know? Bet against what everyone is bettin' for."

"And you?" Vanessa asked.

"You can bet your ass I'm bettin' on you. I studied those tapes you submitted. I ain't ever seen speed like yours. You're gonna make me a fortune. Do you realize that? Most of the funding for this thing comes from the tributes people pay me from their winnings."

Vanessa allowed herself to enjoy the flavor of the cigar and then took a deep breath. Her composure gave off a vibe of assured and calculated.

"So, the prospect of a main event involving either myself, Danny, or Vincent is driving your next big payday, is what you're saying?"

"You're damn right about that." Georgio leaned against the platform.

"What happens if Danny and Vincent meet up in the first round? The fights are randomized, are they not?"

"Vanessa." Georgio narrowed his eyes. "Do you really think I'd risk letting that match happen outside of the main event? I'm a promoter first and a lover of fighting second."

"You're gonna put them in different brackets?"

"Different brackets. They either meet in the final, or they don't."

"Then I want you to put me in the same bracket as Vincent."

"Excuse me?" Georgio narrowed his eyes again.

"I entered this thing for two reasons. To protect Danny from Vincent and then to be crowned the best fighter in the fuckin' world."

"I can't set up every match. Some of them's got to be randomized. People will know I play around with the brackets!"

"Perhaps I just don't enter then."

"What?!" Georgio's cigar nearly fell from his hand while he stood upright. "But you're going to make me so much damn money!"

Vanessa shrugged.

"You're crazy, Vanessa. Damn crazy. The hell's your logic in this? I like you and Danny personally. To be honest, I even like Vincent. However, if I'm going to give you a favor, then I need to know what's in it for me."

"Even more fuckin' money. You put Vincent and me in the same bracket but at opposite ends. When we both make it to the semi-finals, it'll be the biggest payday you've ever seen. Imagine that scenario of back-to-back fights. Vanessa versus Vincent and then the finals, Vanessa versus Danny."

"Or Vincent versus Danny in the finals," Georgio said. "Anything could happen. Either way, the three most anticipated possibilities maximized to the most energy."

Georgio smiled widely.

"The fights will all be legitimate, as you know," Georgio said. "Don't get overconfident. If I do this, you still have to make it to the semi-finals to guarantee this doubleheader."

"Do you really think anybody is going to stop Danny, Vincent, or me? You know damn well we're the best."

"You seem quite certain of yourself," Georgio said.

"Certain enough of my plan to shake on it."

Vanessa reached into her pocket and pulled out a wad of cash neatly clipped together. She kept it hidden near her until swapping it with Georgio in a handshake.

"I seem quite certain of your abilities too." Georgio's eyes widened.

"I want all the fights to be legitimate," Vanessa said. "I want to earn this. I want to fight for this like everyone else, just to be clear. I'm not asking you to fix any of the fights, and I know you wouldn't anyways. I just want to make sure I have the opportunity to knock out Vincent before he cripples Danny."

Georgio slid the money into his pocket and put his cigar back into his mouth.

"Vanessa. The odds are against you. You better prove to the world that Georgio Moroder is the greatest promoter of all time. Kick some ass in this tournament and make me a richer man. Okay? Your wish is granted. If you make it, it'll be you and Vincent in the semi-finals."

Vanessa started to walk away and then turned back around. "Georgio. One more thing." Vanessa said.

"Shoot."

"Talk to me about Raphael Johnson."

Georgio squinted, "The guy from Bassakru? He's an incredible Tae Kwon Do fighter. His tapes were impressive. He looks a little beat up if you ask me, but I read somewhere Bassakru's in a damn civil war with those nasty Xing people, so maybe he's an ex-soldier. That's about all I know. Why?"

Georgio's body language and demeanor did not change. Vanessa got the feeling he was telling the truth.

"Just curious, is all. Pleasure doing business with you."

They both nodded as Vanessa walked toward the exit.

Steam blew from a pipe connected to a concrete wall in the city alley. The rare chilly May night in Chicago caused Vanessa's breath to show itself in the air. Her coat was peppered by the misty rain.

Through the open door in front of her, she said her goodbyes to Georgio. The door closed behind her, and she stepped forward onto the puddle-filled concrete. She looked back and forth through the alleyway. The moonlight glared against the fire exit stairs on each side.

Alone she spoke out loud, "The top fighters in the world come to the worn-out allies of Chicago to prove they're the best. I'd hate on it if it didn't give me inspiration. No flashy lights, no expensive cameras, and no press. Just fighters out to prove they are the best."

Vanessa walked around the puddles of water while staring into the night sky. The lone star escaping through the light pollution amazed her. Amongst the sounds of running pipes, cars in the distance, and little rodents rummaging through garbage, she felt at home in the city. Her mind was on Vincent, and then it was on the sound of footsteps.

To my back, left and right, and another in front.

She continued walking forward as if she was oblivious to the sounds of the environment.

Tap, tap, tap, she heard once more. She did not let her head move in any direction, only her eyes which did a quick peripheral surveillance. The dumpster just ahead of her was the perfect hiding spot and not for her. The moonlight's glare against the fire exit stairs on the other side of the ally was interrupted twice. Her heartbeat began to pick up, and she felt the blood flow to her arms and legs.

The fight or flight reflex that would send most people running simply gave her more focus. She immediately grew irritated at herself. She was a woman in Chicago walking by herself in a dark alley. She shouldn't have had to worry, but society would blame her for being there rather than the ones who targeted her.

She surveyed her surroundings. She noticed metal garbage can lids struggling to contain overflowing trash. A mirror lying against the dumpster and the puddles of water gave her an extra pair of eyes if need be. The moonlight gave away the shadows.

All of her mental work was soon greeted by the slick voice of a tall and flabby man in trashy overalls. His eyes could have been mistaken for yellow in the night, Vanessa thought. He stepped out from behind the dumpster, his body leaning with each step.

The usual teeth-revealing smile grew on his face, "Hey, cupcake. Dangerous part of town. You need help findin' where you're going?"

Vanessa's eyes narrowed, "I'm good, thanks."

Her reply was short and to the point. Unlikely to draw him away, but anything to save her from the situation was worth trying.

Her hopes were dashed by another voice from the side of her. His was high-pitched, "Oh, come on. My boy's offering you help, and you can't even look him in the eye?"

Vanessa turned her eye to him. In a room, the floor would probably shake as he walked. He was no stranger to fast food, and Vanessa took note of his round size. His companion was short and scrawny, staying ten feet behind, forming a triangle around her. She noticed red Xs tattooed on their knuckles. *These are Xing followers.*

The overall-man's voice grew deeper, "Yea, what the fuck? What, you don't want to talk to us? My name is Nick. See, we ain't strangers now, are we? So, talk to us?"

"No," Vanessa replied. Having eyed all the tools her environment gave her, she decided to halt where she was. The puddle in front of her gave her a silhouette of the chubby man behind her.

Nick spit on the ground, "You know what? I was givin' you a chance to be our friend. Guess you don't want that, you rude bitch. Maybe we'll just take that coat of yours and that watch too."

The chubby man belly laughed. "Nicky, I don't think that's all we want to be takin' if you know what I mean."

Vanessa would have rolled her eyes if she didn't want to keep the men in her sight. She blew out a huge sigh of frustration while her shoulders drooped for a second, "Okay, guys, look. I really don't want to do this right now. How's about we just all go about our night?"

Did these Xings recognize Vanessa as an operative, or was this just a typical mugging? She was unable to answer that question herself.

Nick took a few steps closer to her, "Sorry. You really got no choice in this matter."

Vanessa again pleaded, "Guys... Please listen to me. I really don't want to do this. I am not in the mood."

Chubby smacked his hands to his chest, and all of him jiggled. "Oh, come on. I think you'll like it. Just give us a chance. We ain't bad guys or nothin'. Just friendly. You're a pretty girl, and we could really show you a good time."

Vanessa shook her head, "But your guy Nicky wants to rob me."

Nick forced a big smile while taking another step closer, "I'm only playin' maybe... Maybe you just have a good time with us."

Vanessa kept her ears locked onto the third, who still stood in place. Chubby's reflection had not altered in the puddle, so she knew he had not moved.

Chubby once again shouted, "Fuck this bitch, Nicky. She ain't down with us. I wonder what she looks like under that coat."

Nick twirled his head, "Care to let us find out, Miss... What is your name?"

Vanessa raised her eyes and her voice, "Okay, you know what? Last chance, guys. Let's not do this."

Nick shrugged, "Too late."

Vanessa let out a chuckle. "Too late for who? Let me tell you about the type of night you're having, okay? You and your friends are trying to assault a woman who spends her days hunting down terrorists and killing them with her bare hands. I'm a trained fighter. So, I am fucking telling you one last time, I do not want to do this. I am going to count backward from five. You have until one to turn around and go about your business."

Chubby barked, "Oooo, she's a feisty one!"

Vanessa counted, "Five." The scrawny man did not make a move still. Chubby took a step closer.

Nick laughed, "Five's a crowd, honey."

Vanessa counted, "Four."

Nick replied, "Four's just right."

Vanessa kept the same expression, "Three."

Nick took a step closer, "You're serious about this?"

Chubby chimed in, "I got her booty, Nick. You get her front. Think the carpet matches the drapes?! Ha!"

Vanessa continued, "Two." She took a step closer to Nick.

Nick put his arms out, "You actually approaching me?"

Vanessa finished, "One…"

Nick's smile was erased, and his eyes flared, "Who the fuck do you think you are, you scrawny little cunt? Going to blow me off? Let me guess, you're one of those equal rights skanks, aren't you?"

Vanessa slowly shook her head, "Now that's no way to talk to a lady."

"Fuck off," Nick hissed. "I'm the fucking king around here!"

When Nick reached out toward her, Vanessa's instinctive training came in. She moved faster than the blink of an eye. Her hands wrapped around his forearm while she pulled him forward. He was four inches taller, but her quickness and firm grip took him off guard. His body tilted forward, and her heel shot up, smashing into his testicles. His face turned red, and his screams echoed throughout the ally.

Vanessa spun her body around, releasing hold of Nick. The momentum sent his chest crashing against the dumpster while his head dropped into the inside of it. She made a quick sprint for the dumpster lid and swung it downward. Nick felt a thud against his head, and then another, and another, his legs kicking out with each one. His yellow teeth were painted red by the impact.

"Nick!" Chubby shouted. "I got you!"

Vanessa watched his stomach jiggle with each step of his exhausting sprint. He weighed triple her weight, and a simple punch to the face would be a waste. The distance between them shrank to near zero as he threw his hands out to grab her. She tossed her arms forward and bent her body, rolling under his grasp. Splashes of water stained her coat as she rolled through the puddle and back to her feet, grabbing hold of the trash can lid.

Chubby's head bopped back and forth as he struggled to catch his breath, "You-You fucking bitch!" he screamed as loud as he could.

He turned around, preparing for another charge. As his head turned, it was met with the sickening thud of metal against it. Vanessa pulled her arm back and, in milliseconds, swung again, striking him the same as before.

"Ow!" he cried out as he threw both fists out in blind attempts for a hit. She leaned back, the first punch swinging past her. The second punch came for her, and she jumped back, evading. She held the lid like a Frisby and swung. It spun through the air and cracked into Chubby's throat.

He let out a gargle of pain and hugged his throat in a reflexive attempt to control the pain. She shot both legs sideways, landing in the splits on the ground. She balled up her fist and swung forward. The pain in his throat was nullified by the extreme numbing of her fist slamming into his testicles. His high-pitched voice grew high enough to crack glass. He froze in place as Vanessa grabbed the garbage can lid, lurching to her feet. She raised it into the air and swung sideways. The lid cracked against his head. His mind slipped into unconsciousness, and he tumbled to the ground in a puddle of dirty water.

Nick had one hand over his head with his teeth grinding and his breathing becoming rapid. "You scrawny little shit!" he screamed.

He ran toward her, his arms swinging through the air. He shot a straight punch at her. His speed was nonexistent, and his form was sloppy. The second it took for his arm to move through the air was a lifetime to a trained fighter like Vanessa. She had both hands around his forearm and pulled him forward once more. She raised her heel and shot downwards into his shin. The impact shot through him like a tidal wave, and his bone snapped. He became weightless as his nervous system went mad trying to contain the pain. His screams turned to a waterfall of tears as he collapsed to the ground, his head cracking against the concrete.

Vanessa let her shoulders drop as she breathed a sigh of relief. She heard sporadic rapid breathing. Nick was in the fetal position on the ground, and Chubby was out cold. She turned around to see the scrawny man staring at her.

The knife in his hand may have felt threatening if it wasn't accompanied by the panicked tremble of terror. "I...I...Who...You..." is all he could mutter. His eyes were wide open, and his shoulders shook so hard they looked ready to pop off.

Vanessa pointed her hand toward his friends, "Really?"

His trembling was now accompanied by his skin's transformation to pale. He tossed the knife to the ground and turned. His footsteps grew quieter the farther he ran away.

Vanessa looked down at Nick writhing in agony and Chubby lying motionless. Her senses were hit with a terrible smell coming from Nick. She knew what that meant.

She reached into her coat pocket, "You wanted my stuff? Here's a few napkins," tossing them down, "wipe your ass."

She stopped at the mirror lying against the dumpster. She ran her hands threw her hair, combing it behind her. She dusted the dirt marks off her coat. Did these Xings target her intentionally, or was it a coincidence? It didn't really matter anymore. They were destroyed, and she didn't have a scratch on her. She gave her coat one final tug before moving along.

A minute later, she was getting into the passenger side of Danny's car. She closed the door, and Danny looked at her, shaking his head, "What took you so long?"

Vanessa pulled down the mirror in front of her to fix her hair again, "Oh, a couple of guys tried to mug me."

Danny's eyes bulged open, and he leaned in closer as his jaw dropped, "Are they okay?"

Vanessa shrugged, "They'll recover. I called them an ambulance."

Danny nodded, "Alright then. Maryse and I are hungry. You down to eat?"

Vanessa replied, "Let's do it."

CHAPTER EIGHT

Danny sat alone before the skyline of Chicago with the waters of Lake Michigan crashing against the harbor. The crisp smell penetrated his senses. The sounds of boats, waves, and happy chatter dominated his hearing. He watched the cars traveling across Lake Shore Drive in the distance. The sun painted dusk across the lake with its own beautiful reflection.

Danny was alone with his thoughts and his memories. His mind was drained by all of the people around him because it made him hypervigilant. He thought maybe enough time away from combat would alleviate this issue, but it did not. He did his best to enjoy the views anyways. Danny had not learned how to readjust to civilian life, and the United States Government did not bother to teach their soldiers how to navigate this process.

Raphael Johnson walked up next to Danny, breaking his concentration.

"I must be honest, Danny Richmond," Raphael said. "I was very nervous to introduce myself to you."

Danny squinted and turned, "Excuse me?"

Instinctively Danny wanted to keep his hand near his gun until he remembered he no longer carried one. *Shit.*

"I have heard a lot about you," Raphael said. "My brother tells me you are a warrior."

Danny took note of the man's tattoos. He also noticed the exhaustion plastered across his body. The bags under his eyes and the scars across his skin gave away some of his life story.

"Who am I speaking to?" Danny stood up, and they nearly matched in height.

"Forgive my manners." He laughed. "My name is Raphael Johnson."

"You Bassakran?" Danny asked.

"What gave it away?"

"Your tattoos." Danny politely smiled. "How can I help you?"

Danny remained guarded. He could tell Raphael was nervous, but his body was too exhausted to express it. How did Raphael know him?

"May we sit down again, please?" Raphael asked.

Danny nodded, and they sat down on the steps overlooking the skyline. Danny knew Raphael was in the tournament, and that is the only reason he felt comfortable enough to sit down with him.

"Bassakru has a lot of really beautiful views like this too, Mr. Richmond." Raphael waved his hands across the skyline. "You should see Sapo National Park and Buchanan City. Sapo is just beautiful. Green as far as the eye can see. Wildlife everywhere. And then Buchanan, the buildings and houses against the water. I love spending time there. Did you know Bassakru is one of the cruise ship capitals of the world?"

"Bassakru is a cruise ship capital?" Danny said with a smile.

"Oh yea, many companies register out of Bassakru due to its point in the Atlantic Ocean. Not too difficult to get to Europe from us either."

"Did you live in Bassakru as a kid? When did you move to the States?"

"Born, raised, and lived in Bassakru since birth. Bassakru also has one of the youngest populations in the world. Our median age is seventeen and eighteen years old." Raphael looked directly into his eyes.

Danny stared back at him. They both knew the topic they were dancing around. Danny tapped his knee, hoping it would be avoided altogether.

"Bassakru's also known for its fashion, too, isn't it?" Danny asked.

"Yes," Raphael smiled. "Fashion, like in America, is a big deal there. My Dad used to love riding his motorcycle with his aviator sunglasses on. I miss him a lot. He used to have a saying. Every time an old man dies, it is as if a library has burnt down."

"What happened to him?" Danny asked.

"He was a prominent journalist and openly protested the Xings coming to power," Raphael said with a straight face.

Oh fuck. Danny thought. It was as if Raphael was staring into his soul. Danny was being forced to do the last thing he wanted to do. He had to face the reality of the world.

"Then the regulatory committee censored his talk show," Raphael continued. "Our house was condemned by the government for 'code violations,' forcing us onto the streets. After that did not silence him, his car was 'accidentally' struck by a drunk driver, and he died. My mother spoke out and got food poisoning, which killed her shortly afterwards."

"I am sorry..." Danny said. "I don't get it. I thought Bassakru's democracy was growing. The civil war ended a while ago."

Raphael appeared slightly offended and had every right to be. Danny knew what he was saying was nonsense. When would he just face reality?

"We were," Raphael said. "But the Ebola outbreak changed everything. Our healthcare system broke down. And then a few sudden violent uprisings of unconfirmed origins triggered a further economic crisis."

Raphael stopped for a second to let his words sink in, "Slowly, officials influenced by Xing ideology started to win elections and appointments based on fear. Xings hold a supermajority in our Senate and House of Representatives. The President is a proud Xing. You see, Mr. Richmond, Xings used democracy to break democracy. They took advantage of crises that they manufactured and swooped into power by advertising themselves as saviors. Democracy no longer exists in Bassakru... It is an illusion. We have been under a fascist regime for some time now."

Danny's eyes began to water. He knew more about the crisis in Bassakru than he said out loud. Raphael could sense it.

"So why did you come to the States then?"

"There is another saying in Bassakru. A little rain each day will fill the rivers to overflowing."

"Meaning?" Danny asked.

"For me, it means the Xings may have powerful resources, but if all of us stand up, they cannot contain us. That is why I am here. To make you an offer and ask for your help."

"My help?" Danny kept a straight face, but on the inside, his heartbeat increased.

"I'm not asking you to be a soldier again. I am asking you to consult or, at the very least, speak to your contacts and convince them to help us."

"Okay, listen, Raphael. No bullshit. Before this conversation goes any further, I need you to say it outright. How do you plan to fight the Xings?"

Raphael sat upright with pride, "I am a leader in the Bassakru Resistance against the Xings. There is a new Civil War in my country. We do not harm innocent people, and we do not bomb civilian targets. We aim strictly for Xing officials and Xing military."

"How's the fight going? How is morale? I mean, talk to me, big daddy."

For a split second, it seemed as if the old Danny Richmond was breaking free. He was trying to construct a visual in his head of the entire situation.

"Not good," Raphael said. "Our fighters are strong, educated, and determined. However, most never wanted to be soldiers. Before the Xings took full control, they were teachers, doctors, taxi drivers, farmers, and market workers. We are low on supplies. We do not ask for your troops; we just need the resources to keep going. Some who resist disappear."

"Jesus, that's terrible," Danny said.

"Yes." Raphael nodded. "My brother said you were strong. That if you got involved, you could get us the resources to help us turn the tides of this conflict."

Danny tapped his knees and then stood up. He looked around at all the families moving about in bliss. The United States flag waved off the top of multiple boats that sailed across the lake.

Helping Raphael was the right thing to do. Danny was trained to help those in need. This could even give him what he has been lacking since he became a civilian. A mission and a purpose.

"I can't help you," Danny said while staring off at the skyline, "I'm sorry." He avoided eye contact with Raphael.

"You-You won't help? I don't understand."

"Listen, maybe if this were a few years ago, I'd be down for this challenge, but, to be frank with ya, it just ain't me anymore. Ya dig what I'm saying? I'm looking for a job. I have a girlfriend I have to answer to. It's a whole thing, ya see? I have a house to take care of." Danny kept his hands on his hips to hide that one was shaking.

Danny could not escape the turmoil he was feeling. How could he help Raphael fight the Xings when his psyche was in shatters? The remaining twenty-five percent of the puzzle was still in that pile on the floor.

"I don't believe what I am hearing. Danny, people are dying, being murdered on a mass level. Our natural resources. Timber, gold, iron ore, diamonds, rubber, are being stripped away from us.

"The people of Bassakru are well educated and ready to stand up. They very much believe in democracy. We can accomplish this with just a little bit of resources. Are you really going to say no?"

Danny said nothing and kept staring away.

Raphael looked up and down at Danny's luxurious clothing.

"That gold watch," Raphael said. "How much did it cost you?"

"A lot of money. Why?"

"In my country, some might call you a Shikii. It's a person who dresses in high fashion and acts like the boss. Shikiis are said to want the whole world to believe they have money, even if they don't. They're known to use their last penny to buy a gold watch or chain." Raphael took a deep breath. "Tell me. Do these clothes and Wall Street make you rich? Or is this all a bluff?"

Danny's eyes widened. Raphael' words pierced through his soul. Danny had done everything he could to run from the nightmare in his mind. So, what if he acted like a Shikii? At least this way, he never had to deal with the pain.

"Raphael," Danny said, finally looking at him. "You just crossed a line. Can't say I appreciate your accusation."

"Accusations? You're worried about accusations while people are being oppressed and slaughtered by the Xings? Not throwing around accusations, I promise. I'm merely trying to understand how my brother could tell me stories about you, the mighty warrior who crushed dictatorships, only to find he is a man who actively runs from the fight."

"Runs from the fight?!" Danny threw his hands into the air. "I have had enough of this! Why the hell did you come to me with any of this?! Who is this brother you're talking about?! I bet it's some conning CIA operative. Quick piece of advice: Operatives are known for lying and playing roles. It's a big part of what they do for a living. You may want to ask your brother about his agenda."

"My brother is a fighter. I trust him with my fucking life. As to why I came to you? Because I believe the stories he told me about you. If my words today do not sway you, then I must tell you. I too, am entered into the Golden Dragon Tournament."

"The fuck you enter in that for? How in the world is that going to help you fight the Xings?"

"By winning and earning your respect. Perhaps if you see my resolve, you will be persuaded to join the fight."

Danny ran his hands through his hair. He wanted to say a million things but had no way to verbalize them. His moral conscience was in conflict with the mental illness ravaging his brain.

"I'm..." Danny finally made eye contact with him. "I'm sorry. I really am. Believe me, I do respect you. I respect everything you stand for. I just... I can't be of help right now. I'm on my own journey right now. My own fight."

"I also have something you couldn't say no to," Raphael said. "A bargaining chip. Something that I know you will want." Raphael went to reach into his pocket in a quick motion.

"Keep your hands away from your pockets!" Danny threw his hands up and started walking backward. What the hell did Raphael have in his pocket? Danny remembered how many enemies acted like his friend during the day and then tried to kill him at night. It happened on every mission. It made trust a dangerous game.

Danny looked around at all the strangers amongst them. Why did they have to crowd him? Were any of them with Raphael? Was this an ambush like on so many missions?

"I have to go. Okay?" Danny said in a quick tone. "Hope to spar with you in the tournament. Take care."

"Please wait!" Raphael said without taking the hard drive out of his pocket. It was probably best Danny never saw the hard drive because his anxiety was already out of control.

Danny was turned around and speed-walking away before Raphael could say anything else.

Danny picked up the pace. Suddenly the large crowds around him felt threatening. The numerous cars sitting idly by were suspicious. He could feel the anxiety coming through every part of his body with no escape.

The crowds reminded him of a wave of enemy soldiers flanking his position. The vehicles reminded him of the car bomb that took out a fellow operative, Jason, on a past mission. The explosion had given Danny light burns but had scorched Jason. Just a minute before the explosion, Danny and Jason had switched spots. Jason's body shielded him from the blast.

And then his heart started racing out of control. Danny's blood was rushing, and his breathing became constricted. Why the hell were people loitering around the entrance to the parking lot? Danny took the long way around to his vehicle to avoid them. There was no guarantee of who they were.

Danny made it to his car with his anxiety in full control. The horrors of war were fresh in his mind. Everything around him acted as a reminder. He grew angry. He sat in his car with the doors locked and closed his eyes. He started focusing on his breathing and remembering the words from a past counselor. He followed her direction to a tee in hopes of coming out of this sudden battle with as few scars as possible.

Danny wanted to help Raphael, but how could he when he was fighting a losing battle in his mind?

CHAPTER NINE

The noise of crowd chatter filled the amphitheater arena. In the front rows were couples wearing their most expensive clothes, not shy about their expensive watches and diamond earrings. The farther up the seats, the more casual the clothing was. The ages of the audience spanned from eighteen years old to seventy. The smell of blood and sweat had become a staple of this arena, and it did not fail to deliver the atmosphere.

Danny sat in the front row of the fighters' bleacher seats diagonal from the platform. All around him were the fighters in this tournament. He stared around at the audience, taking in the whole environment.

Danny made eye contact with Raphael. Danny was still feeling the ripple effects from their previous encounter. It numbed Danny's guilt and kept him focused on calming his own mind. They nodded to each other. Looking back at it, Danny knew Raphael meant him no harm, but how could he have been sure of that? So many others in the past had tried to stab him in the back.

Vanessa leaned into him, "Has it always been this simplistic? I don't mean that as a bad thing either."

Vanessa brought upon a most welcomed interruption from his obsessive thoughts. Danny was positive she recognized his struggle and was trying to pull his mind out of it.

"Yep," Danny said. "The only spectacle focused on is the one that takes place between the fighters. There's no need for fancy jumbotrons, fireworks, news networks, or glitzy lights. Look up there." Danny said.

Danny pointed to the ceiling, and Vanessa observed. Hanging from the ceiling were the flags of each country being represented in the tournament.

She noticed how the platform, in the center of it all, dominated the room. The audience stretched like a U-shape around the platform. To the north of the platform was the Master of Ceremonies desk, where the honorary head of the tournament, Yoshi Toroko, sat. He was clothed in a martial arts Gi, his belt notched and adorned with more stripes and accolades than most people even knew existed. To each side of him were other legendary fighters well into their sixties like he was.

The digital read-out board was plastered against the wall behind them. It appeared to be the only thing in the room that had been built in this century.

Vanessa asked, "Are you ready for this, Danny?"

How the hell was he supposed to know? They were interrupted anyways, as Peter had the ability to shout even when he wasn't yelling.

"This is going to be fucking awesome, man," Peter said.

"Think so big man?" Danny said.

"I know it. Can you feel the electricity of the crowd? We are about to make history! We have a saying for the biggest event in wrestling. The showcase of the immortals. That's what this feels like."

"You're like a kid in a candy store," Vanessa said. "You're really amped for this, aren't you?"

"Damn right I am! Vanessa, I say after we finish here today, we go on a skydive or something crazy like that! Keep the blood flowing!" Peter spoke with his hands.

"I ain't see you this happy since you started dating your wife back in high school," Danny said with a laugh.

The happy presence of Peter was destroyed by the voice of one man, "Danny boy... It's been a long time."

Danny quickly turned around to stare Vincent in the eyes. He clenched his fist in anticipation. The flashback of their last battle ran through his head yet again. It was Vincent's crazed look of aggression that replayed itself the most.

Danny replied, "It has. Not surprised you wouldn't challenge me to my face."

Vincent hissed, "Well, there are rules about fighting before the tournament. The Vin Man didn't want to disqualify himself by hurtin' ya too early. We got a paying audience to entertain."

Danny took a step forward but was unable to put his feelings into words. Staring back at him was his brother. They knew all of each other's secrets, triumphs, and fears.

Danny wanted nothing more than to get his brother back, but Vincent only grew more enraged with each attempt.

"You don't have the slightest clue what's coming to you," Vincent said. "I have waited for over a decade for this. Not that you would know. Can you even fight anymore? Hell, can you even think anymore? Mr. brain damage, right?"

Danny remained silent while staring into Vincent's eyes. The more Vincent talked, the more tense their muscles grew. Vincent took a step closer to Danny.

Vincent continued, "Nothing to say? Come on. Hit me back with one of them Richmondisms. Maybe throw some money at me, so I go away. Run and hide. It's what-"

Vanessa stepped in front of Danny and stopped centimeters from Vincent's face.

"Who the fuck do you think you're talking to?" Vanessa said.

The tension reached a fever pitch. Danny immediately put himself in between them and backed Vanessa away, "Don't let him get to you."

Vincent laughed, "Look at that! You got your girl fighting your battles for you now?"

Vanessa shot back, "How's about we start the tournament early, punk, and I knock your ass out now?!"

Vanessa was not immune to fear. Having Vincent so close put her in serious danger, and she knew it. Regardless, the fighter in her loved the thrill.

Vincent winked, "See ya in the tournament, Danny boy. I'll finish what I started last time." and walked up the bleachers to his seat.

Vincent's words were the ultimate trigger that broke another memory of their last fight free from its repression.

Vincent's heel cracked into Danny's throat. Danny hugged the area of impact with his hands. He felt the blood rushing in that reduced his air supply.

Vincent grabbed Danny's wrist and kicked towards his leg. Danny yanked free and lurched backward. Danny's feet left the ground as Vincent's heel smashed into Danny's shin. There was a loud crack that accompanied Danny's barrel roll through the air. Danny was covered in swellings and blood. His bones screamed in agony, and his body now lay on the edge of the platform. Blood clogged his throat. With one eye swollen shut, he stared at Vincent. Vincent stared down at him, his chest rising and falling rapidly. His eyes were glossy, and his lips were shut. His face was without remorse.

A loud gong sounded. It rang every few seconds and sent vibrations through their souls. Yoshi Toroko stood up from his chair, holding a microphone. He observed the crowd that reached a little over a thousand. He looked to the fighters all congregated on the bleachers and to the audience.

"Welcome all. Today is Round One of a tournament that is sure to test the will of all thirty-two fighters who have entered. All of the fighters have proven to be some of the best in the world. On the platform are the screams of pain and determination of hundreds of warriors over the last twenty-one years. Their blood, sweat, and tears have permanently changed the color of the mat they fight on. Thirty-two fighters from over twenty different countries are represented in this tournament. Over a hundred have been represented in the past three decades. The rules are simple. Each match will contain two fighters with no time limit. The match only ends if a fighter is knocked out, submits, or is knocked off the platform. The tournament will proceed in every other day intervals, with the main event taking place by itself on the final day. We will now bow our heads in silence as the gong is rung ten times to honor the fighters who have come before us."

Every head bowed, and everyone closed their eyes.

The first gong rang. Danny dug into his training to keep his heart rate in check. Everything in his life had led him to this moment. He had to fight his own brother just to stand up to his demons. The time was now upon him to find out if he still had the Dragon Heart spirit.

The second gong rang, and Vanessa's mood remained unchanged. Vanessa had a mission to accomplish, and she wanted to become the best fighter of all.

The third gong rang, and Raphael thought of Bassakru. Each gong represented comrades slain by the Xing Empire. He pictured the Xing's ugly red flag with the golden X waving in the wind like a never-ending nightmare.

Vincent sat in silence. His head full of rage and memories. He thought of his history with Danny and everything they had been through. It all brought him back to this moment.

The time for fighting was now upon them. Little beads of sweat had already found their way onto the heads of each fighter. No amount of training could ever hold back the nerves that the Golden Dragon Tournament forced. If the rules had not forbidden it, this tournament would have had a body count to go with it. The honor, the glory, and the affirmation of being the best was the foundation of the tournament's prestige.

Georgio Moroder sat next to Maryse in the front row. She observed her surroundings. The fans, the fighters, and the ring. All of it combined gave a barbaric feel, and she was beginning to understand that was the point. In this room, humans were transported back hundreds of years. The transformation was so complete it started to seem like modern conveniences like key fobs, cell phones, and electricity were out of place while the ancient architecture, traditional garb, and the barbaric rituals seemed to be what truly belonged.

The digital board sprang to life. Round 1, Match — Vanessa Rodes (USA) Vs. Julius Serenity (Honduras)!

The crowd immediately began to clap. Vanessa's entrance into the tournament generated almost as much buzz as Danny and Vincent's possible showdown.

Danny looked to Vanessa, "You got this. Watch out for his reach."

"Thank you." Vanessa gave a quick nod.

Vanessa made her way onto the platform, standing across from Julius. His six-foot-six, slim body gave him a towering advantage over her. He had to stare down to look her in the eyes. She stared up at him, unwavering and unafraid.

"Come on. "Julius said. "Can't you smile for me?! You always look so angry! You know we don't have to fight. I'll take you to my room, where we can have a different type of match."

The referee placed his hand in between them, signaling the match was only seconds away from starting.

Vanessa remained expressionless and focused. She ran her eyes up and down his body, searching for any weak spots not well-conditioned.

Maryse immediately leaned into Georgio, "Mr. Moroder, what should I expect of this fight? What are Vanessa's chances? Who is this, Julius?"

He leaned toward her while keeping his eyes on the fighters, "Julius is a wild fighter from Honduras. Brutal too. I don't know what to make of this fight just yet. Big size, reach, and weight difference between these two."

"Have other women been in this tournament before?"

"Just one. She was an undefeated kickboxing champion before entering the Golden Dragon."

"And?"

"She lost in the first round. She got crushed."

Maryse felt her heart sink. Her concern for Vanessa would have been noble if it were based on her well-being. If Vanessa failed to beat Julius, then Danny would probably end up facing that Vincent fighter. She didn't think anyone could actually hurt Danny in this tournament, but the thought of him in any amount of danger did not sit well with her.

The referee looked to Vanessa and then to Julius. Julius continued to smirk. If he was waiting for Vanessa to smile back, he was going to be disappointed.

"Fight!" the referee shouted as he swung his arm up and stepped back.

Vanessa placed her right fist to her side and her left fist out in front of her. She circled the platform. She hopped two inches off the ground nonstop while seemingly gliding around the platform in a technique called shifting.

Julius placed both arms out in front of him, palms facing forward in a Muay Thai stance. Vanessa circled around him once and then a second time. Each time she eyed his body movements as he followed her in a circle. She stayed in place in front of him, making direct eye contact.

He chuckled, "Oh come on… Big me versus little you? Last chance, princess. You know-"

Vanessa sprang to life, swinging her right leg diagonally for a spear kick. Julius had a muscular upper body and wobbly legs. She capitalized on his weakness. Her shin smacked against his hamstring, and before he could register the pain, she struck again with the same kick, and then again, and again. Julius' upright stance turned into a crooked L shape as he struggled to keep his balance.

She hammered into his hamstring with five more roundhouse kicks. She raced toward his ankles and wrapped her arms around them. She yanked back, and he faceplanted against the platform. She released, and he pressed his hands against the floor to rise. With his knees buckling and his body bent over, Vanessa swooped in. Her knee zipped upward while her hands squeezed his head. Her knee smacked against his nose, which gave way to a loud crunch.

The crowd could feel the impact from their seats and gasped in awe. She followed up with more rapid knee strikes. A second, a third, and a fourth that left blood squirting from his nose as his eyes flooded with reflex tears.

A fifth knee strike to his nose sent his arms flapping around.

The crowd gasped again.

A sixth knee strike caused the same reaction and sent more blood splattering across her attire. The white platform was painted with a new blotch of red.

Vanessa stepped back and turned sideways. She shot her leg out in a spear motion for a sidekick. Her heel cracked into his temple and wobbled his head in all directions. The glaring lights of the amphitheater turned black for Julius as he slipped into unconsciousness. His body plopped to the ground.

The referee rushed in to check on Julius, and Vanessa began to scream, "Come on! Get up! Let's go! I thought you wanted to take me out to dinner, you little bitch!"

The referee threw his index finger up, pointing toward the officials to signal a victory by knockout. His gesture was followed by a loud gong that announced her victory. The crowd scrambled to their feet, clapping. Most could not process what they had just witnessed. A few men in the front row shook their heads in disgust. Vanessa was not their enemy, the amount of money they lost betting against her was.

Vanessa turned till she had direct eye contact with Vincent.

Vincent had a smirk on his face, and his eyes were focused on her. He felt a thrill from the entire situation. Fighters were not allowed to bet on the matches, but if they were, he would have put all his money on Vanessa in that one. She was called the fastest gun in the west for a reason.

Vanessa calmly walked back to her seat. Paramedics raced in to carry Julius off the platform. She sat next to Danny, who handed her a rag to clean off her clothes.

Danny had a serious expression, "Fuckin' dynamite."

"That was a rush. He left himself wide open. Julius must have suffered a recent leg injury because they weren't well-conditioned. Unusual for a Muay Thai fighter. He underestimated me."

A series of fights occurred through the hour that kept the crowd amped. Each fight added a few more bloodstains to the platform. Danny, Vanessa, Vincent, and Raphael all paid close attention to each fighter.

The digital read-out board sprang to life once more. Akira Naraku (Japan) Vs. Danny Richmond (USA). The crowd roared. The bets started piling up quick to the anticipated return of the man whose name was once synonymous with the tournament.

Danny did all he could to hide the nerves that ran through his body. He wished he had continued his ongoing mental health therapy to help him remember. Still, he did not know how to open the door. He was going in less than 100 percent, and he knew it. So did Vanessa. His biggest fear was Vincent picking up on it.

Vanessa said calmly, "Take it slow out there, Danny. Don't be foolish."

Danny simply nodded and stood up, making his way to the platform. Her advice was the best he could get. He stood across from Akira on the platform. Akira was a few inches shorter with a stockier build. His buzz-cut hair and puffy cheeks would not give him a menacing look in street clothing. Danny knew better than to underestimate a fighter, as Julius had just learned the hard way.

Akira smiled and said in thick-accented English, "You're Danny Richmond? I remember what you did to my father in this tournament. Now I'll settle the score for him."

"Sincerely hope your pops is doing well, Akira. Give him my hello. As for us... No holds barred, buddy..."

Danny and Akira respected each other, but both were determined to win at any cost.

Maryse leaned into Georgio, "Who is this, Asira?"

"Akira, you mean. He is a newer fighter. His father's participation in past tournaments helped get him here. He's younger but no slouch. He has an awesome win-loss record."

Maryse didn't think much of it. Danny didn't look scared to her after all. If he was so calm, then she was certain victory was imminent.

The referee held his hand in between them. Danny could not escape his thoughts. Danny thought of the time it took him to learn to walk again. He thought of his ongoing memory issues. This was supposed to be the impossible moment, yet here he was.

Danny had one fist near his side, the other arm bent in front of him, his hand open like a claw. Akira had a similar stance. The referee looked both of them in the eyes and then threw his hand up.

As soon as the word fight left his mouth, Danny began to circle the ring, as did Akira, slowly moving in closer to Danny. Danny's heart started to pound, and he had to grind his teeth to keep his face expressionless. Any sign of weakness he let Akira see would only embolden him to go for the kill. Any weakness he let Vincent see could lead to his defeat later. If he made it to later.

Vincent remained locked onto Danny. Rarely blinking and moving a muscle even less. He had just as much invested in this match as Danny and Vanessa.

Danny and Akira closed in on each other, spiraling toward striking distance. Danny swung his fist forward for a straight punch. Akira threw his forearms up and then felt the clip of Danny's fist against his jaw. His head snapped back, and Danny felt a small wave of confidence. He still had his speed.

He heard his father's voice roar into his head, "One hit means nothing! Focus!"

Danny swung his leg around for a sidekick, striking Akira in the thigh. Akira's body dipped sideways as Danny threw his fist forward for another punch. Akira went airborne and placed both feet together. He aimed downwards, and his dropkick collided into

Danny's ankle like a rocket. It caused Danny's arms to flail as his body fell forward.

Akira landed on his hands and feet. Akira shot a kick backward as Danny fell. Danny's cheek met with Akira's heel. A mist of blood exploded from Danny's mouth and he was sent barrel rolling through the air.

Vanessa bit her lip, watching the series of events. She knew the man who trained with her years ago would have never let that happen so early on.

Lying on his back, Danny wondered if he was in over his head. He forced his thoughts back into focus before Akira could capitalize. Distraction was how you got your bones broken in this tournament.

Akira wasted no time and quickly moved in on Danny. Danny began to roll sideways and placed his hands to the platform to rise. With his fists clenched, Akira raised his leg up and shot his heel down. His foot stomped into Danny's lower back. The kick sent Danny back into the platform. Akira executed another stomp more concentrated onto Danny's lower back. Danny's muscles tightened with pain. Danny masked his pain because he refused to give Akira the confidence booster.

Danny forced himself to roll over quicker than last time. The safety of the center platform was gone. He was now on his back and meters away from the edge. He placed his palms against the mat. Akira approached him cautiously, knowing Danny could trip him out of the platform. His hesitation was Danny's plan, and it gave him the second he needed to kip-up to his feet.

Vanessa's heart skipped seeing Danny so close to the edge. She knew it was a huge risk.

"Damn it..." she mouthed.

She noticed Danny's heel nearly hanging off the edge of the platform. She bit her fingernails in worry. The crowd responded with a gasp of anxiety and excitement because the match was one hit away from ending.

Without hesitation, Akira swung a straight kick at Danny. The crowd did not help Danny's confidence but grew Akira's. Danny threw his fist down and knocked the kick away. Danny orchestrated a right hook. Akira threw both forearms up, knocking it away.

Akira then shot back with a kick at lightning speed, Danny knocked it away with his fist and went for a kick of his own. Danny could feel the platform's edge with his heel. The danger filled him with adrenaline and fear, which could be a blessing or a death sentence.

They continued to exchange punches and kicks. Each deflection was met with a sickening smack that echoed loud enough for the entire audience to hear. Akira lurched into the air and placed both feet together. It all happened in seconds. Danny scouted Akira's dropkick and shot his body sideways into a roll. Akira's feet shuttled over Danny's body and found nothing but air. Akira landed on his stomach and rose to his feet while Danny came out of his roll, standing in the center platform.

Akira ran toward Danny to escape the suicide of the platform's edge. Akira screamed at the top of his lungs with his eyes wide open and his teeth out like a lion roaring at its prey.

Danny roared back at a higher decimal, "Bring it, you son of a bitch!"

Akira shot one leg forward, followed by the other in a bicycle motion. Danny hopped back and evaded. Danny kneeled down and swung around with a leg sweep. Akira hopped to evade. Danny rushed to his feet, and Akira shot his foot upward and then back down like an axe. Before Danny could fully stand, Akira's heel swiped across his cheekbone. A sharp pain shot through his face as he fell back first onto the platform. Akira once again brought his fist to his chest as he raised his foot and slammed it down. His foot cracked into Danny's sternum. Danny had never been hit by a car, but he didn't imagine it felt much worse than that kick! Akira's move was calculated as the sternum was a universal weak spot.

Akira repeated the kick. Danny attempted to roll away and was laid flat by Akira's kick into his shoulder. Akira raised his foot again, aiming for the sternum. Again, Danny tried to roll, and Akira's kick kept him on the mat. Akira lifted his leg, and the process was repeated with similar results.

The pain was becoming unbearable. Danny knew if he did not escape soon, Akira would hit him with a finishing blow.

"Damn it, Danny." Vanessa mouthed. "Come on. Get out of there."

Vincent said nothing to himself. He only noted the weak points on Danny's body. Focusing on each spot where his expression showed he incurred the worst pain.

Akira stepped in closer to Danny and raised his leg up for the final blow. Akira shot down with all the force in his body, and with no other option, Danny rolled toward the kick rather than away. Akira's foot cracked into Danny's shoulder. Danny gritted his teeth to absorb the pain as he wrapped a forearm around Akira's ankle with the other hand pushing against Akira's foot to rotate it. Danny was kneeled on one knee while applying the submission hold.

Akira could feel his ankle breaking and the heart-stopping pain in his bones. He shook his leg up and down in a desperate attempt to break free. Danny had just enough strength over Akira to keep his hold locked in.

Danny pushed Akira's foot further into a dangerous direction. Akira knew he was only inches away from a full-on ankle break.

In desperation, Akira shot his free leg forward and let his body fall. His heel headed toward Danny's face like a rocket. Danny relaxed himself and leaned his head back to let his jaw take the impact. Akira's heel connected. Danny roared with a long-lasting war cry that vibrated across the amphitheater. In one action, he absorbed the pain and struck terror into his opponent.

Danny kept hold of his ankle lock maneuver. Akira was now on his stomach with his palms against the mat. Akira planted his hands and foot against the platform in an attempt to rise up.

Danny dropped to his back and wrapped both legs around Akira's leg in a triangle formation. Akira's body crumbled flatly onto the platform, with the weight of his opponent anchoring him in place.

Danny knew Akira did not have the strength to escape, and with his adrenaline rushing, he screamed at the top of his lungs, "Akira, give up!"

"No!" Akira screamed as he pounded his fists against the platform in fury.

Danny twisted Akira's ankle further. The bones started to crack and pop.

Danny screamed at a higher decimal than before, "I'll snap it, you son of bitch! You know damn well I will! Submit now!"

Akira's face was bright red in agony, and he did not have the strength to break free. It was over, and he knew it. For another ten seconds he held on, searching desperately in his mind for a miracle comeback. Each second that passed was another second less he had to walk away.

His pride gave way to the reality of his demise, "I submit! I submit!" he cried out in embarrassment.

The referee pointed two fingers in the air toward the judges to signal a submission. The gong rang, and the crowd rose to their feet in applause. Even those who had bet on Akira clapped out of respect for the bout.

Georgio had a large smile on his face, "Danny is going to make us a fortune this year! The money we gain from all the betting! Oh my!"

Maryse's eyes widened in disbelief, "You are smiling? This excites you? My Daniel could be seriously hurt! My God, that was barbaric!"

Vanessa pumped her fist in victory and relief.

Vincent remained expressionless and motionless. Silently taking note of all the important takeaways from the fight.

CHAPTER TEN

Danny bowed to the masters of ceremonies and then made his way back to the bleachers. Had he been in private, he would be massaging his shoulder and sternum. Doing so now would give his opponents, especially Vincent, a bullseye to focus on. He simply did what the best fighters do and acted as if he was perfectly healthy. The pain in his body would have to wait until he was in bed. He sat next to Vanessa, who handed him a rag to wipe the blood from his face.

"How you feeling?" Vanessa asked, already knowing the answer.

"Like I got hit by a freight train."

"Akira's a good fighter." Vanessa shrugged. "But you should have been able to end that in half the time while incurring less than half the damage."

"Roarin' Tiger." Danny felt his aggravation grow at the truth. "I hear ya' loud and clear. Fuck, it hurts to talk."

Over the next half an hour, another slew of fights went on, each of which wowed the crowd in different ways. Raphael Johnson came out victorious in his fight with a spinning heel kick that left his opponent unconscious. Danny, Vanessa, and Vincent all paid close attention to each fighter in preparation for battle with them. Vanessa stayed on the lookout for anything suspicious. With each passing fight, the crowd grew more boisterous, but when the digital read-out board sprang to life, reading Vincent Diezego (USA) Vs. Peter Jacobs (USA), the spectators collectively reached a fevered pitch.

Vanessa looked to Danny. She knew from the way he clenched his jaw that he was nervous. Vanessa's shoulders sank into her chest.

The boisterous crowd grew into a rumble of whispers. Vincent's name now dominated the conversations. Vincent Diezego had been the reigning champion longer than anybody in the tournament's history. He left a trail of broken bodies in his wake. He was the odds-on favorite to win it all again.

Peter Jacobs rose from his feet. He looked to Danny and Vanessa as if he was fighting to contain his excitement. His smile was impossible to hide, "Ladies and gentlemen, boys and girls, and children of all ages, get ready for the grandest fight you have ever seen!" Peter threw his hands up into the air, and the crowd nearby responded uproariously. Though he had never participated in the Golden Dragon Tournament, he was perhaps the most well-known competitor, having wrestled on television for years.

"Peter," Vanessa said.

"I've worked hard every night and day..." Peter sang, smirking as he interrupted her. Neither Danny nor Vanessa laughed, but he continued singing a classic movie tune.

He elbowed Danny gently, trying to get him to join in.

"It's a mistake to make a joke out of this," Danny said.

"Are you calling epic movie songs a joke?"

"Peter," Vanessa hissed. "This is the real deal. No choreography out there."

"Come on, laugh! It's funny!" Peter slapped Danny on the shoulder.

Peter turned to walk away, and Danny grabbed him by the wrist. Danny's eyes were watery, and his expression stern.

"Peter, listen to me, okay?"

Peter rolled his eyes.

"Stick and move," Danny continued, making direct eye contact. "Stick and move. Don't try to stand and bang with him. You can't win against him that way. He's a bigger guy, which means endurance will be an issue for him. Outlast him."

"Relax, brother," Peter said, brushing him off. "I've got this. Do you know how many fights I've been in?"

Danny let go of Peter, and then Vanessa stood up.

"Back out now," Vanessa said.

"What?" Peter asked, throwing his arms out.

"You fuckin' heard me."

"Not a chance. I grew up with Vincent too. I ain't scared of him," Peter said.

"Listen to me, damn it!" Vanessa said. "I know you're as tough as they come. You're a professional wrestler, for Christ's sake! But this is different! What you're doing is suicide!"

"Vanessa, I can take care of myself!" Peter said.

"No! You fuckin' idiot!" Vanessa shouted, causing heads to turn in their direction. "You need to back out now! Fake an injury, feign illness! I don't care! Just don't go into this thing! Vincent is going to crush you in there! This is not a damn game anymore! Do you understand me?! This is real life!"

"Vanessa... Trust me. I got this." Peter stared directly into her eyes. "I love you, but you really do come off like the strict parents from an eighties teen movie. Relax."

Peter patted her on the back and then walked toward the platform.

Vincent stood on the platform with his fists to his side. His V-shape body was amplified by the extreme definition across his body. He wore boxing shorts with his last name stitched down both sides.

Peter stood across from him, wearing camouflage boxing pants and a matching bandana. He noticed the smell of sweat permeating from the platform.

"Tell me," Maryse said, leaning into Georgio, "who is this Vince fellow? Why do so many seem to fear him?"

"Vincent is an awesome fighter," Georgio said. "He's won the last few years in a row, crushing every opponent who gets in his way. Majority in the betting pool are throwing their money toward him in this fight."

"And you? What do you think will happen?" Maryse asked.

"We will see. I do not know Peter Jacobs all that well."

"Vincent does not look that much bigger than Peter," Maryse said. "Peter appears to be really confident too. Maybe Vincent is not the threat some are making him out to be."

Maryse shrugged and leaned back in her seat.

Peter's smile was big enough for the audience in the top row to make out.

"Good ol' Vinnie DZ! How you been, brother?!"

The referee started to make his way over to them.

Vincent narrowed his eyes.

"Oh, come on. No response? DZ, do you remember when we were all real little kids, and I beat you in that game of tag? Do you remember how you got all mad afterwards?"

Vincent lightly chuckled but remained still with his fists hanging down.

The referee stood in between them. He looked at them both and then signaled for the fight to begin.

In the bleachers, Vanessa could not sit still. Danny kept his eyes glued onto the fight while biting his lip.

Vincent got into a traditional southpaw boxer stance. Peter got into a similar stance with one arm perched back farther than the other. The crowd immediately came to life.

"Now the fight's on," Vincent said without a smile. His eyes looked remorseless, with the veins in his arms bulging out of his skin.

They both circled the platform at different paces. Vincent was calm and moved only in inches. Peter seemed to hop with each sidestep. In only seconds they had entered striking distance.

Vincent executed a straight punch, and Peter evaded. Peter threw a right hook, and Vincent knocked it away with his forearm.

Peter attempted a left hook, and Vincent blocked with his elbow. Another punch from Peter and Vincent knocked it away. Peter increased his speed with each punch. The routine seemed to continue on forever. Peter threw one punch after the other, with Vincent evading each one.

Peter's eyes grew wider with each deflected hit. He seemed to sweat a little more.

"Is this really your best?!" Vincent laughed.

Danny's heart sank. *No. No. No. Get out of there.*

"What are you doing?!" Vanessa shouted. "Are you a fool, Peter?!"

"He's doing the exact opposite of what we told him to do! He can't go strike for strike with him!"

Vincent's chuckle turned into a boisterous laugh as he knocked away every strike. Peter felt his humiliation-fueled anxiety starting to build. The entire crowd was watching him fail to land even a single punch. Vincent's mocking only further enraged him.

"You son of a bitch!" Peter shouted.

Peter picked up his pace while grinding his teeth. Sweat started to bead down his face as he swung at full speed.

"Someone getting mad now?!" Vincent laughed. "Remember when we were in high school, you wanted to spar with me, and I made you tap out in fifteen seconds like a little bitch?!"

Peter went for a swift straight punch. Vincent leaned back to evade it. Peter arched for another punch, and Vincent simply stood with his arms to his side.

"You can't even hit me. This is pathetic," Vincent said.

Peter started to swing his fist, and Vincent threw up his elbows to protect his face. Suddenly Peter's entire body went into motion as he sprinted forward. In a split-second, Peter's body speared into Vincent's like a freight train. Vincent's back met the floor with Peter mounted on top of him. The impact echoed throughout the amphitheater.

Peter executed a swift punch that clocked Vincent in the face. He repeated with a second, a third, and then a fourth. Each one hitting harder than the last. The crowd began to rise to their feet, with their cheers growing in anticipation. The momentum had just shifted, and everybody felt it.

Vincent shot his right fist upward for a powerful punch. Peter latched onto it with both hands while falling onto his side. Peter pulled Vincent's arms between his legs. Peter locked in an armbar and started bending Vincent's arm backward. Peter tightened his hold like an anaconda, gripping tighter and tighter with each passing second.

Vincent wanted to roll out of the submission but feared breaking his own elbow. Everyone in the entire amphitheater was now on their feet.

"Holy shit," Vanessa said, standing. "Is he actually going to win?"

"I don't fuckin' believe it," Danny said in amazement.

The crowd's disbelief was expressed through the roar of excitement. Was the underdog going to prevail? Was the professional wrestler going to finally unseat the undisputed champion?

Georgio smirked and could not take his eyes away.

"Listen to this crowd. What a turn of events we have here!" Georgio said.

"This Vince is not so tough after all," Maryse said with a smile.

"Tap out! Tap out now, you scumbag!" Peter roared at Vincent. "Tap out before I break your fuckin' elbow! I have the hold locked in! You can't escape without me snapping it!"

The referee kneeled down by Vincent, "Do you submit?! Do you submit?!"

Peter's sweat from earlier had only gotten more intense. It started to run down his arms and cover his hands.

Vincent led with his legs and started to slide his body counterclockwise to escape the hold. Peter wrapped both feet over each other and pressed them into Vincent's chest to keep him at bay. Peter cinched in the hold a little tighter, and Vincent felt the pain increase.

Vincent could feel the sweat from Peter's hands that weakened his grip. Vincent slid his head underneath Peter's legs while pushing them off. Peter threw his leg back over Vincent in a chopping motion. Vincent's body collapsed back into the mat with Peter's legs across his chest again.

Vincent knew it was time for untraditional tactics. He placed his other forearm against the top of Peter's foot and began to push down with every bit of strength he had. Peter's bones began to stretch, and he kicked down at Vincent. Vincent rose his free fist into the air and slammed it into Peter's shin.

"Ah fuck!" Peter screamed while his hand slid down Vincent's arm from the sweat.

Vincent repeated the same attack. Peter screamed and felt a numbing sensation. Vincent repeated this strike multiple times, and each one loosened Peter's grip.

Peter released one hand from the armbar and shot a punch at Vincent. In the blink of an eye, Vincent forced his body upward with all of his momentum until he was sitting up. Vincent slid his body across Peter's in a counterclockwise scramble. With the sweat building and Vincent's wild moves, Peter lost his grip. Vincent stopped with one knee on the ground and the other digging into Peter's stomach. With Peter stuck on his back, Vincent arched his arm back and hammered his fist down. Peter felt the force of a boulder crashing into his right ribcage. A sharp, tweezer-like pain followed a sickening crack that reverberated throughout the amphitheater.

In a panic, Peter pushed Vincent off of him. Peter rolled away and rose to his feet. He put his fists out in front of him and his body crumbled forward. The pain in his ribs had become excruciating. Every breath he took felt like an army of razor blades dancing across the sides of his body.

More pronounced than the pain was the look of terror in Peter's wide eyes. Vincent rose to his feet, twirling his arm around with a smirk on his face.

Danny sighed and closed his eyes for only a second. He took a deep breath and opened them.

"It's over," Danny said. "Peter needs to give up."

Peter threw a straight punch, but Vincent pre-empted the attack with a thrust kick, shooting his heel forward and cracking it into Peter's ribcage. Peter staggered, and Vincent executed a saber-sharp sidekick to Peter's ribcage.

Peter began to back away with his breathing growing more rapid.

"What happened?!" Vincent threw his arms out. "Why are you running now?! Come on! Tell me another joke!"

"I would never run from you!" Peter charged forward like before and ignored his pain.

It happened in rapid motion; Vincent snapped his heel upward into Peter's head, followed by an uppercut into his jaw. Vincent then speared another thrust kick into Peter's solar plexus. The smacking sound of the impact was sickening.

The crowd gasped in unison as Peter leaned forward on reflex. His stomach turned into knots while his lower legs started to feel numb. His chest tightened uncontrollably, and his head jerked with each breath he struggled to take. He coughed, and a line of blood spurted from his mouth. Peter hugged his injuries with his consciousness slipping away.

"I-I-I can't breathe!" Peter struggled to speak. His lungs gasped for oxygen. "I'm suffocating! I'm suffocating!" he tried to yell. His words only came out as tiny whispers. Peter's expression cried panic.

Peter started to fall forward, and Vincent wrapped his hand around Peter's neck to keep him standing.

"Feel that pain? Like you can't breathe?" Vincent continued with a whisper into Peter's ear. "Feels like you're suffocating, right? I hit your solar plexus, which has concussed your phrenic nerve, temporarily shutting it down. Which means for the next thirty seconds, your diaphragm can't contract to give your lungs oxygen. It's a universal weak spot. I believe an untrained idiot like you would call it getting the wind knocked out of you."

Danny rose from his seat and shouted loud enough to be heard, "Damn it, Peter. Submit! Live to fight another day! Please!"

Danny's hand began to tremble. One of his childhood friends was on the cusp of catastrophe. A few forgotten memories with Peter from their childhood slipped back into Danny's consciousness. He remembered Peter's smiling face at that time and how contagious it had been even decades ago. The smile was nowhere to be found in the present. The memories quickly reminded him of his own struggle.

Peter made a split-second eye contact with Danny. Danny could feel Peter's regret and humiliation. Peter's face was bright red with swelling.

Vincent cracked another right hook across Peter's face while never letting go of his neck. Vincent followed with another hook to the same area. Vincent released his hold and executed another volley of hook punches that sent Peter's head snapping back and forth. Vincent kept a smile on his face through each strike. Every time Peter began to fall forward, Vincent struck him in the head.

Peter gargled and threw a punch in desperation. Vincent caught it in his fist and squeezed tightly. Vincent snapped another heel kick into Peter's ribcage. Peter's agony was audible over the noise of the crowd.

"Damn it, Vincent, you son of a bitch!" Danny screamed. "Just throw him off the platform! You've won!"

Vincent kept hold of Peter's arm and pulled him toward the platform's edge until they were both facing Danny and Vanessa.

Vincent pointed to Danny.

"This is going to be you, motherfucker!" Vincent said.

Vincent put his palm out and arched his arm all the way back. He pulled Peter's arm straight and made direct eye contact with Danny. Vincent swung his palm forward at lightning speed toward Peter's elbow. There was a sickening crack as blood splattered across the platform. Peter's elbow had snapped into a compound fracture that left his bone protruding out of the skin like a skyscraper in a cornfield.

Vincent released Peter and let him collapse onto the platform. Peter could not contain his screams or his labored breathing. Peter cried for help in between his screeches. Vincent stood over Peter as calm as ever, with his eyes never leaving Danny's.

The referee threw two fingers into the air signaling Vincent's victory by submission.

Danny and Vanessa both rushed onto the platform where Peter lay.

"Get this man some help!" Danny shouted, climbing onto the platform and kneeling by his friend. "It will be okay. Just relax," Danny tried to whisper to Peter.

Paramedics arrived with a stretcher and, within no time, took Peter away.

The crowd had fallen to near silence. Though the audience paid to see violence, they expected all in the tournament to fight within the code of honor. Vincent had gone too far to prove a point, and his barbarism left many fans disgusted. Most in the audience shook their heads and looked away as a sign of disrespect.

Vincent swaggered across the platform and came face to face with Danny and Vanessa.

"You son of a bitch!" Vanessa shouted. "You could have won that match from the moment the bell rang! You didn't need to do that!"

"I could have easily won in the first ten seconds," Vincent shrugged. "But then I wouldn't get to see Danny boy over here stewing in primal rage!" He laughed.

Danny did not say a word because he knew any attempt to speak would lead to him throwing fists.

"What's wrong?" Vincent got nose-to-nose with Danny. "You mad at me now? I bet you'd love to strike me down for what I've done. Wouldn't you?"

Danny gritted his teeth and remained speechless. His face was red with rage. He could feel the eyes of everyone in the amphitheater trained on him and Vincent.

"Hit me," Vincent smirked. "Do it! Come on! Hit me!"

Danny wanted to do so much more than just hit him but knew the consequences would be his disqualification.

"Just what I thought," Vincent said. "A fuckin' coward as always. How pathetic." Vincent shook his head and walked away toward the locker room.

Danny walked off the platform near the locker room entrance, and Vanessa followed. He paced back and forth with his hands trembling. The visual of Vincent's final blow to Peter was too similar to the final blow from his last bout with Vincent, and he couldn't help but remember. The horror of Peter's screams blended with the humiliation of his heart from all those years ago.

Vanessa's breathing was fast-paced as she lifted her finger at Danny, "This is why you can't fight him, damn it!" she shouted, "Do you get it now?! He is a monster now! You remember what happened last time!"

"Shut up!" Danny turned to her raising his finger in return, "I can fight him! I'm not afraid of him! I've got the heart of a Dragon running through my veins, you got that?!" His words betrayed his true feeling, which enraged him further, "I am Danny Kyle Richmond, son of Thomas Richmond! I have saved the fuckin' world, and I'm going to fuckin' prove to you and everyone else that I am still the man I used to be!"

"Excuse me?! Don't you ever tell me to shut up! Who ya' trying to convince, Danny? Me or yourself? Huh? Lose that macho bullshit with me. I see right through it."

Danny was preparing a fiery response but was cut off by the clacking of high heels marching in his direction. He turned to see Maryse's bright red face with tears streaming down her cheeks.

Danny forced a calm demeanor and stuck his arms out, "Maryse—"

She swung her hand out, and the smack across his face echoed like a shotgun blast. The impact left a receipt across his cheek.

Maryse went off in a rage-filled rant in French. She transitioned to English to ensure he processed every word. Her hands moved through the air as she raved on, "You barbaric, idiotic man! Is this the type of tournament you want to be in?! This tournament is sickening, and so are the fighters who compete in it! Are you a mad man?! How can you call yourselves honorable in the face of such atrocities?! Vincent should be behind bars, and you should be in a looney bin for even wanting any part of this barbarism!"

Danny threw his hands out, "Maryse, calm down! Alright? I know what I'm doin'. This is about my honor. I have to know – "

"Your honor?!" Maryse screamed as she took another swing at him and connected hard.

She cocked her hand back and went for a third slap. Danny zipped his hand up and wrapped it around her forearm. He squeezed tightly as he placed his finger in front of her with his face red with fury, "Don't. Ever. Do. That. Again…"

"What the hell is wrong with you, Danny?!" Vanessa screamed at him as she yanked Danny's grip away. Maryse pulled her arm back and caressed it. She turned away, unable to stop the tears from rolling down her face.

Vanessa gently placed her hands on Maryse's shoulders for support and whispered, "I'm genuinely sorry. Are you okay?"

Maryse threw her hand up to push Vanessa back and stomped away.

"And you're ready?" Vanessa slowly shook her head while staring at Danny, "To fight in this tournament? To fight Vincent? Is this how you find yourself? By becoming him?"

Danny's eyes remained glued to the floor as a million emotions ran through his body. He buried his face into his hands.

Vanessa leaned in and spoke in a low volume, "I'm going to do all I can to take down Vincent before he can get to you and cripple you. I don't know where my best friend has gone, but I sure as hell hope you find him again because the Danny Richmond I knew is not here..."

Vanessa walked away to leave Danny alone with his thoughts.

CHAPTER ELEVEN

It was two in the morning, and traffic on Lake Shore Drive was light. Vanessa drove to match the flow of traffic around her. Maryse was in the passenger's seat. The city was quiet, with the ride smooth and slick. Vanessa took comfort in the wind blowing through her hair. With the top down, she could see the Chicago skyline on one side and Lake Michigan on the other.

"Nice night, isn't it? I love the city lights at night. Don't you, Mar?"

Maryse stared at the city horizon. The beauty of the city was the farthest from her mind. Like a car wreck, Vincent's destruction of Peter did not leave.

Vanessa asked, "Want me to play some music? I got all types of genres on my phone."

Maryse responded the same as before, with nothing.

"Look," Vanessa continued, "I'm really sorry about what Danny did and how he acted back there. I know how shocking all of this must be to you."

Vanessa took a moment before plotting her next move. She enjoyed the sounds around her. Cars zoomed past with gusts following in their wake. She could hear the lake's water brush against the shoreline. Colors of red and white headlights dotted the streets as far as she could see. The skyscrapers dominated the horizon, while Lake Michigan's endless beauty relaxed her. Even though she had been all over the world, nothing ever hit quite like home.

For a moment, her mind took her back to only two years ago when it would have been her and Danny in the car. The routine was so much simpler then. Eat, train, CIA missions, sleep, and repeat. They took drives like this together during their downtime to cool off. They would discuss the next mission, break down the issues of the world, and plot their next move. Now that felt like a lifetime ago.

The quiet night would have been heaven for her if it had not been for the tension with Maryse. She was determined to break it for her own sanity.

A smirk came onto her face as she stared at Maryse and then back to the road. She took a deep breath and spoke part of a sentence in perfect French.

Maryse's head finally left her palm, and slowly she turned to stare at Vanessa, finishing the sentence in French.

Vanessa translated their French back to English, "Little by little, the bird makes its nest."

"Since when did you learn French, Miss Rodes?"

I was on a mission in France. Vanessa thought. No matter how much Danny trusted Maryse, Vanessa never forgot the importance of secrets. Additionally, she wasn't sure if Maryse would believe she saved the President of France from an assassination attempt.

Vanessa continued, "I've made my way over to France a few times. I know a few languages. My French isn't perfect, mind you."

Maryse felt a little awkward. She had made a lot of malicious remarks about Vanessa to her face. All of which Maryse had thought Vanessa didn't understand. None of which she would take back now, even if she were asked.

Maryse asked with little emotion, "So, you understood everything that I have said in front of you?"

Vanessa knew what she was referring to, "Everything."

"I am impressed. Not many Americans can balance multiple languages."

"I'm full of surprises," Vanessa said. "Anyways, I really am sorry about how Danny treated you."

"Do not be. It is not anything you can prevent. He is a man who, for reasons that bare no logic, would allow his elbow to be ripped from his body to prove he can be a fighter."

"It's not just about being the best fighter. It means so much more to him, to me, and all the other fighters in that tournament. Maryse, this is Danny trying to hang onto who he was before all this.

Before the money, banks, Wall Street, and the big house. He was different then."

Maryse rolled her eyes. She looked at the five-figure watch on her wrist and then back to Vanessa. "I do not understand the honor in the life he lived before. You two have never been an item, is that correct?"

Vanessa could tell that Maryse was asking to quell her own jealousy.

"Never," Vanessa said, trying not to let her emotions show. Admitting the truth deflated her, though. Danny was the man she loved, and no matter who she dated, he was one of the few she truly ever felt right with.

"Our old routine," Vanessa said, "Was eat, missions, train, sleep, and repeat. It was all about the job. The job is still my life."

"So that is all you do? Is fight?" Maryse asked, her curiosity kindled. "All the past eleven years? You do not get lonely? I do not understand. It sounds like a life with needs unmet and a lot of bloodshed. I can think of a million better ways to spend time."

Vanessa was not sure if Maryse was being spiteful or sincere. For her own sanity, she assumed the latter.

"Oh, trust me. I get my needs met when needed. Traveling all over the world makes that easy enough. I have dated, had boyfriends and girlfriends. Even had a long-term relationship that went years, got engaged to him. With my background and lifestyle, most men feel their masculinity too threatened by me to stick around long. Me being away for months on end doesn't help either. Sort of stupid. I had some relationships that barely lasted because a guy would do things to challenge my strength. Total acts of insecurity to massage their bruised egos. None of them would ever admit to their intentions, but I could sense them. There was the one, Ethan, who I was engaged to. He and I were really tight, and he treated me wonderfully. We came razor close to tying the knot, but sadly, things didn't work out with him.

"In terms of Danny, he competes with me in fighting, but it's out of the thrill of the challenge. It's for the purpose of trying to better our fighting abilities. Danny always understood me and the poor background I came from. He's been my biggest supporter. Not that I needed his encouragement, but he would always encourage me to shove it in the face of anyone who looked down on me. And believe me, being a woman in the line of work Danny and I are in, I had to work twice as hard, accomplish twice as much to get the same amount of respect."

Maryse's path had been so much different, though. Her path was filled with every luxury since her birth. Her rise to the top of the modeling world was made easier by her mother running one of the largest modeling agencies on the globe.

Maryse pressed further, "Tell me more about yours and Daniel's past together."

"He was more selfless. I can't put it into words. I never felt comfortable spending a lot of money because I never used to have it. So, I save everything and buy only the necessities. He was like that too, until he eventually started to change. We were really close those days. We spent almost every day together sometimes."

"Listen to me, Miss Rodes and listen good," Maryse said, narrowing her eyes and pointing at Vanessa. Her tone resembled a mother speaking to her children, "Daniel Richmond is my man. Do you think I am blind? I speak the language of love and can see the look you two give each other. So, I am going to make this clear: Don't try anything with him. Do not think I fear you just because you can break a man's nose. I will not have my boundaries stomped on."

Vanessa squeezed the steering wheel until it creaked as a way to let out her anger. Maryse's attitude ate at her for so many reasons. She could fold Maryse into a pretzel, but Maryse knew Vanessa would never throw the first punch. Maryse was the kid taunting the caged lion at the zoo.

Vanessa looked Maryse in the eyes only for a second and then put her focus on the road, "First off, you don't need to take that tone with me, nor are you going to. I'm not going to get in the way of you and Danny." *For now*, she thought.

Vanessa continued. "I think we both know you should have tried talking him out of this damn tournament."

"You are right on that one. I will give it to you."

Vanessa was surprised that Maryse conceded, "You and I have our own lives, anyways. I don't wait around for him or anybody."

"Fair point," Maryse said, "So, tell me, why are you in the tournament? Why risk the injury? And do not take that as an insult. I am genuinely curious."

If only Maryse knew Vanessa was in the tournament on orders of the United States Government. Vanessa thought it best to leave that part out.

"My initial reason was to prevent Danny from getting crushed by Vincent. But an even bigger reason is that I want to win. To have the honor of being the greatest fighter in the world is huge."

Maryse stared at the city skyline for a moment and noticed how beautiful it was. She turned back to Vanessa, "Okay then, explain this to me. You are a highly intelligent person. I have seen that in you from the first time I met you. How does someone so smart find herself into a life like yours? I mean to find a thrill in fighting? Why?"

Vanessa took a deep breath. She was so used to keeping everything a secret. For the moment, she decided she would let her guard down. She needed to talk about it, and Maryse already knew too much anyway.

"Maryse, when I was a kid, the seventeenth of every month was grocery shopping day. Do you know why?" Vanessa asked.

Maryse shook her head no.

Vanessa continued, "It's when my parents got our food stamps in. My parents had to make every dollar stretch. I usually missed school field trips because I didn't want to bring home the permission slips and make my parents feel guilty when they would be unable to pay the fees. I hate talking about it, actually. We never talked about our financial perils with family or friends. We were always ashamed. I'd go to sleep over at other friends' houses in different neighborhoods and be amazed at the air conditioning being on all day during the summer. We only used ours when company was over."

Vanessa paused for a moment to collect her thoughts, "My parents used to tell me we were playing hide and seek when the doorbell rang. As I grew older, I realized they were hiding from debt collectors. Leaving the phone disconnected was often for the same reason. I was working by the time I was fifteen years old because I got tired of duck-taping over the holes in my shoes or having to sow together torn clothes. My parents loved me and my siblings unconditionally. They would skip meals to be sure that we ate. They would skip doctor visits to ensure they had money to take us."

Vanessa flicked on the turn signal and changed lanes. Talking about these past memories made her a little emotional. She decided not to hide it from Maryse.

"Why did your family not have money?" Maryse asked.

Vanessa gulped to suppress the harder emotions, "My little brother got diagnosed with a near-deadly illness. It threw them into catastrophic medical debt just to keep him alive. My parents both had jobs though, which meant we didn't qualify for certain critical assistance even though we were still broke anyways. We were in that grey area that nobody in America ever talks about. Too much income to be considered poor and too much medical debt to ever have money."

"Tell me more," Maryse said while leaning in.

"Well," Vanessa chuckled. "It built a sense of community in me. My entire neighborhood was poor, so we would usually work together to scrounge up the basic needs. Fix each other's vehicles. You helped a family, and they helped you in return. My parents are honest people, but those medical issues destroyed us financially. Then my dad had a stress heart attack and could not work for many years. Everything compounded."

"It is sure different than my world," Maryse admitted. "I grew up with everything a person could ask for. Honestly, I cannot even imagine having to go through what you did." Maryse was not bragging but simply making an observation, and Vanessa knew that.

"Yes. Crazy, isn't it? We come from different worlds." Vanessa said. "The only extracurricular activity I was ever involved in was martial arts, and that was because a family friend agreed to train me for free as a favor he owed my father. It's where I started my Krav Maga training and got my black belt. Before then, I was lost. I was attending a million parties, getting into trouble with the law, getting drunk, and the rest. It was bad. Martial Arts saved me. Once I graduated high school, I went into the Air Force because the military was the only way I could go to college for free. I wound up becoming a fighter pilot and fell in love with government service. I got my Bachelor's in Political Science while enlisted. I was convinced I would run for political office to fight the injustices my family faced."

Vanessa ran her hand through her hair. She realized Maryse was waiting for more information, so Vanessa continued, "I lived a life surrounded by injustice. My family had nothing. We lived on our parent's love. What I do for a living now, it's how I fight back against the injustice. I get to make the world safer and see justice comes to bad people."

"So, how did you find yourself with the agency?" Maryse asked.

"I can't talk about work too much, but I can tell you. I was recruited to my current job from the Air Force."

"Huh? How?" Maryse squinted.

Vanessa was not sure she wanted to share this with anyone. She looked away for a moment and gulped again. There was a lot of pain Vanessa dealt with too, though she spoke about it a lot less. Vanessa thought if Maryse got to know the real her, they could start to form a real friendship. Besides, maybe it would be therapeutic to talk about it with someone outside of her line of work.

"I was a fighter pilot deployed at base. We were ambushed during a small sandstorm. I got my hands on an assault rifle." Vanessa shook her head as if to clear her own conscience. "One by one, I killed our enemies. A lot of them. The last enemy was getting away with stolen equipment in a truck. The heavy winds were kicking up the sand. The enemy was a few football fields away, making a turn. I picked up a sniper rifle from a dead comrade."

Vanessa took two seconds to compose herself, "I shot a bullet right into the enemy's chest. Word spread about me pretty quickly after that. The agency recruited me just as I was honorably discharged. I met Danny while on the job, and we bonded instantly. He started sparring with me in Dragon Heart martial arts, and everything grew from there."

Maryse could not take her eyes off of Vanessa, unable to speak. Her jaw hung open, and her hand cuffed the back of her head.

"My God," was all Maryse could say.

Vanessa could sense Maryse was now uncomfortable, which made sense. How could she possibly understand a life like Vanessa's? Even though Vanessa's targets were usually terrorists or evil foreign officials, she hated killing. It just happened to be something she had always been good at. It's why the CIA hired her. She was a weapon in the arsenal of democracy.

"You really do not believe Daniel has a chance of beating Vincent but feel you do?"

Vanessa flowed with Maryse's attempt to change the subject.

"I don't know about Danny. He's not himself. He needs a lot of therapy. This is a reckless move on his part. But for now, all of that is irrelevant because I know I can beat Vincent, and I will. He won't have a shot to get to Danny. I intend to prove that I am, without a shadow of doubt, the very best fighter in the world. I promise you that, Maryse."

Maryse said in French, "Chacun voit midi à sa porte."

Vanessa asked, "Everyone sees noon at the door? I don't get what you mean."

"It means to judge a situation based on your own subjective criteria. For Daniel's sake, I hope you can do everything you say you can."

Vanessa clenched the steering wheel once more, "I'm going to do this. Trust me..."

The sounds of the staff and the patients in downtown Chicago's Northwestern Hospital forced its way into Peter's room. Peter was in post-surgery and wore the scars of his battle.

The exhaustion was a lethal enemy for Danny, who sat at his friend's bedside. It was magnified by the fear creeping its way through Danny's body. It was dawn, and the black bags under Danny's eyes was evidence of his lack of sleep. The golden rays of sunlight came through in between the curtains and stripped across the interior.

Danny could not take his eyes off his friend. The usually contagious smile on Peter's face was gone. Peter's arm was wrapped tightly in a cast.

Danny saw Peter's injuries as his own. The tournament was supposed to be his therapy. Instead, it became the same type of nightmare he had spent the last year trying to forget.

I failed. Danny kept thinking to himself. He was supposed to be the protector. He should have known better, but he didn't. Maybe Vanessa was right after all.

Danny's head fell into his hands by the weight of his own turmoil.

"What the fuck happened to me?" Peter barely let out.

"Holy shit! You're awake already?" Danny looked up.

"I feel like shit," Peter said.

Peter looked all over his body. He looked at his elbow, and his eyes began to water. Danny could feel Peter's terror. He could see Peter fighting to calm himself.

"How bad is it? Give me the real scoop." Peter asked.

Danny knew what he was really asking. Peter did not move a muscle. He stared at the ceiling with his jaw clenched shut.

"Miraculously, you'll make a full recovery. Your wrestling career isn't over, but you'll be out for a good while," Danny assured him.

"But-But I can't miss, man. I can't miss!" Peter started to breathe heavily. He closed his eyes and laid his head into his pillow.

Danny felt like trash. How much easier would it be if Peter smiled through this like he did everything else? He waited for Peter's optimistic approach to soothe his own guilt. It wasn't coming, and that hurt Danny worse.

"Damn it! Damn it! Damn it!" Peter shouted. "Damn it!" One tear escaped Peter's eye and flowed across his bruises.

"My career could be over," Peter muttered.

"I promise you the doctors are 100 percent certain you will make a full recovery. I am so sorry for this. I-I-I'm sorry. I should have never let you in this tournament."

"Fuck you, Danny," Peter said. "Don't put this on yourself. It's my fault. Vanessa tried to warn us, but we didn't listen. We got cocky. It's all on me. I volunteered for this. It was my idea."

Peter's words did not alleviate the weight on Danny's shoulders.

"Danny," Peter said. "I was wrong. If you backed out, it wouldn't be giving up. It wouldn't be cowardly. It's okay to back out."

"Back out?" Danny said. "How do I do that?"

"How the hell do you not? Look what happened to me. It can happen to you too. If it's pride you're worried about, forget it. Your pride isn't worth your life."

Every logical fiber in Danny's body told him it was time to back out, and yet he knew he couldn't.

"I can't back out now. I've come this far."

"You are serious?"

"Yes," Danny said. "Vincent's my brother. My Dad raised us together. You know how close we were. I've lost who I am. The hero I was, the fighter. It's all missing. If I back down from this, then what does that make me?"

"Fucking logical!" Peter shouted.

"I have to prove to myself that I can still do it," Danny said. "That I can still be Dragon Heart. I know it seems impossible to understand. Even if I can't beat Vincent, which maybe I can't. Maybe he's gotten too good and me too soft. I will never live with myself if I don't."

Peter shook his head and finally made eye contact with Danny.

"If you're not going to back out, then you need to do something. Are you listening?"

"Yes." Danny said."

"You need to dig down deeper than you ever have before. And then you need to take whatever is going wrong with you and fix it. I saw you in that fight with Akira. You hesitated, you were scared, you doubted yourself. Whatever's holding you back, you need to let it all go. Let yourself remember; do you hear me?"

Danny nodded but said nothing. He never lost eye contact with Peter. Danny wanted so badly to do what Peter said, but how could he? Maybe this was a suicide mission, but at least it was a mission.

Danny had to reckon with reality. He wasn't Dragon Heart anymore. That soldier was locked away in a prison. All he had left were his broken memories and the drive to fight on anyways. Danny was feeling something he did not dare admit to others or even himself. It was the same feeling that told him to run far away from the agency and never look back.

Danny sat alone. The logo of the Dragon Heart Dojo was covered in shadows. The pouring rain and endless city traffic from outside were all that gave sound to the place. The mats and workout equipment stood without life. They had gone untouched for so long.

The stuffy smell of dust and dirt irritated his nose. The outside humidity made sweating inevitable.

He looked at the mirror across the wall and saw the splotches of dirty spots that had gone uncared for.

Danny could not escape his feelings. Every piece of equipment reminded him of the man he used to be. The Dragon Heart dojo was once a renowned place of glory on the west side of Chicago. Danny looked behind him and saw the trail of his footsteps strewn across the blanket of dust.

He got up out of his chair and ran his finger across a punching bag. Dust particles flew into the air, leaving a swipe where his finger had been. Every piece of equipment he touched yielded the same result. He collapsed back into his chair.

Just like me. He thought. The dust was a stark reminder of the person he once was. *No authorization granted*. He couldn't forget hearing the orders from his own Chief of Station given to Vanessa:

Leave him behind.

They left him for dead. Just like they had wanted to leave him and Vincent for dead so many years ago. *Shit. Vincent.*

It was hard for Danny to make sense of the fact that Vincent was once a sensei at this dojo too. The same sensei that just put Peter Jacobs into the hospital. The same sensei that would be aiming to add him to his list of victims with a plan to finish what happened the last time they fought.

How the fuck do I even face him? What do I do? If he could just take down Peter like that. I could barely fight Akira. Damn it.

Danny closed his eyes for a moment. He could have sworn he heard echoes of the past. The sounds of determined students, the smell of sweat and hard work, and the fires of passion. The echoes felt louder as Danny let himself dig deeper into them. More forgotten memories had slipped through his barrier.

Danny, Vincent, and eventually Vanessa were all sensei at the dojo, but in reality, they played more of an administrative role. Because they were off on missions around the world so often, other highly esteemed sensei usually trained the students by following Danny's playbook that broke down the unique style of Dragon Heart Martial Arts.

Danny never forgot when and why Vincent left the dojo. That fact triggered another part of an unwanted memory that he wanted to push back. Despite his efforts, the last time he fought, Vincent came to life again. Danny's heart rate skyrocketed, and his shoulders felt like concrete.

Danny forced his eyes open and ripped himself out of the flashback before it could start. He started to play through the coping mechanisms taught to him by his counselor. He looked around the room to remind himself he was in the present and in a different place than the past. He started to focus on the feeling of his feet against the floor. He could see the dust collecting around his shoes and the dirt spread across the walls. Those reminders of reality only heightened his anxiety more.

He thought back to another tip from the counselor about keeping your mind on something good about your life. *Vanessa Rodes.* The image of her smiling face resonated across his mind, and he did not let that image go. She was smart, strong, and she was his rock. She was everything he needed in a partner.

Danny looked back to the dust on his shoe and thought of the last time he fought Vincent. How would this time be any different? The chair behind Danny tipped over in the aftermath of his posthaste walk to the exit. He stepped out into the humid rainfall and locked the doors behind him, never looking back.

CHAPTER TWELVE

The week saw Vincent demolish most of his opponents in a few minutes with knockouts, submissions, and more broken body parts. The psychological terror he put into fighters was his greatest strength. Vanessa made it through most of her fights with only minor bruises because she moved too quickly to be hit. Her unconventional mix of Krav Maga and Dragon Heart Martial Arts gave her an edge over opponents twice her size. Vanessa had to juggle her matches with tracking Raphael and staying on the lookout for Xings.

Raphael had defeated his opponents with his well-aimed kicks, knife hand chops, and a bold style. He flanked every opponent he faced and overwhelmed them.

Danny struggled with opponent after opponent, accumulating damage to his back, chest, and anxiety along the way. He hesitated in each fight and nearly lost more times than he cared to admit.

The platform's surface became a darker and darker shade of red as the week progressed. No amount of sanitizing and cleaning could fully wipe away the stains of the blood, sweat, and tears from so many fighters.

After a week of intense fighting, they were now in the semi-finals with only four fighters out of thirty-two remaining. The crowd buzzed in anticipation. The amount of money bet had reached new records.

"Have you been watching Raphael, Danny?" Vanessa asked.

"What?" Danny asked, his far-off gaze taken away by her question. "Raphael? Yeah. Definitely."

"Raphael Johnson has stunned a lot of us," Vanessa explained, unconvinced by Danny's assurances. "He really shined in this tournament. Be careful with him."

Danny only nodded. What else could he do? Danny was lucky enough to even still be in the tournament, and he hoped nobody else knew it. Danny was not surprised at how well Vanessa fought.

Vanessa placed her hand on his shoulder, "Danny, you can do this."

Danny again said nothing, and Vanessa stared into his eyes. She saw the fear inside of them.

She thought back to the conversation with his neurological doctor that took place just months after Danny's accident.

"Let it go, Danny. Let yourself remember."

"Vanessa..." Danny said, his eyes beginning to water.
He said nothing more, and it was clear she understood.

"You know that tattoo on Raphael' arm is a Bassakran Resistance tattoo, right?" She asked.

As if hit by a jolt of electricity, Danny came back to life, "Of course I do. You saw it too?"

He was unaware Vanessa had been tailing Raphael when he went to speak to Danny. She knew they had already met.

"100 percent," she said. "There's more to this guy. Be careful in there. Watch his knife-edge chops and kicks. And don't expect him to be conventional. He won't fight dirty, but he also won't be afraid to do what he must."

He took her words to heart. Her intelligence always impressed him.

"His chops have been deadly." Vanessa said. "After what he did to Mohammad in the last round, looks like he almost cracked the guy's collarbone. And he knocked out how many others?"

Before Danny could respond, the crowd roared at the sight of the digital read-out board. Raphael Johnson (Bassakru) Vs. Danny Richmond (USA)!

"Georgio!?" Maryse barked, calling on the irascible man's deep wisdom of fighters. "What do you make of this Raphael?"

Georgio, in his usual seat and comfortable responding to demands as long as they were from beautiful women, gave her his own take. "Raphael is really an astounding fighter. He fights with intensity others don't have. He has technique. This will be good. He's also the master of the Knife Hand Chop. It's been abandoned in modern martial science, but it shouldn't be. It's tough, versatile, and effective. It's one of the deadliest blows without the aid of a weapon. Raphael's ability to conquer it shows his grit."

Georgio did not guarantee a Danny victory, and Maryse noticed.

Danny and Raphael stepped onto the platform and stood across from each other.

Danny narrowed his eyes in respect, "Honored to go toe to toe with you."

Raphael kept his expression stern, "Thank you. My people have fought very hard to resist the Xings. I am saddened you still won't acknowledge this."

"It will be a good fight," Danny said as if he didn't hear Raphael.

"Danny, my country needs your help. Please. I entered this tournament, not for glory, but to earn your respect." Raphael said.

"You put your own body at risk? You could have tried methods other than surprising me on the street." Danny said.

"I did." Raphael shook his head. "I wrote you letters. Do you know how risky that was? I put my life in danger. I made phone calls to you. I even got emails to you. You ignored all of them. No one else in your government would listen." Raphael said.

"I never got them." Danny looked away in shame because they both knew damn well he had received all of them. He didn't have the power to respond to them.

"You forced my hand." Raphael got into his fighter stance. "If the suffering of my people cannot move you to act. Then perhaps earning your respect on the platform will. I do not plan on holding back. I was trained in a street style of Tae Kwon Do."

"I don't plan on holding back either."

"The only way to defeat me is to let it all go and face your fears," Raphael said. "You must embrace your past rather than run from it."

Danny got into his fighter stance.

The referee had his hand in between both fighters. His eyes moved back and forth between them. The referee signaled the match start. Danny and Raphael circled around the ring before taking any steps that brought them closer together. Danny knew Raphael had the ability to defeat him even if Danny was at 100 percent. Raphael had made it to the semi-finals for a reason. Raphael's history gave him the most powerful tool of all: Resolve.

Raphael bounced on the balls of his feet, sometimes high enough to look as if he were jump roping. Raphael had a longer reach than most opponents, and that gave him an advantage. Danny knew he would have to close in and bring Raphael to his level. Danny took the first step forward, and Raphael did not flinch. One step after another, Danny was closing the gap between them.

Danny took another step and felt the tension of the situation build. The clock continued to tick away. The seconds turned to a minute as Danny drew closer.

Danny was about to take the step into striking distance. He knew he would have to be as close to Raphael as possible to take away his advantage.

Raphael kept his eyes on Danny's upper body to predict Danny's first move. Any move a fighter made started with movement in that region. Danny took a split second to observe Raphael' tall frame in search of a weak spot. He found none.

Danny kept stalling for time in hopes Raphael would get impatient and make a sloppy first move. *It's not gonna happen*, he finally realized. *He's too damn disciplined.*

Danny, in his current form, lacked that patience, and Raphael knew it. Danny took a deep breath. *Fuck it, here we go.*

Danny charged into Raphael's personal space. Danny came with his front kick toward his enemy's jaw. Raphael spun with catlike speed with his arm extended out, ready to chop Danny's head off. Danny made a posthaste retraction of his legs and covered his head with his elbows. Raphael's forearm felt the pain from Danny's elbow, and Danny's arm felt the force of Raphael's hit.

Danny swiftly grabbed Raphael's forearm. Danny hammered his other elbow into Raphael' bicep three times in a quick motion. Raphael' body jerked with each strike. Danny knew he had to neutralize Raphael' limbs to achieve victory.

Raphael leaped into the air and cartwheeled over Danny's head. Danny kept his grip on Raphael's forearm the entire time in an attempt to yank it out of socket. The leap distracted Danny, and then he felt Raphael's thumbnail dig into his eye. Danny reflexively threw both hands up to knock the attack away while Raphael landed on his feet.

The attack caused no pain but forced involuntary tears to blur Danny's non-dominant eye. Both of his eyes clamped shut on and off as Danny rushed to clear the tears away.

"Fuck," Vanessa whispered from her seat on the bleachers, biting her lip in worry. "Focus, Danny. Get the fuck away from him to recoup."

She knew Danny well enough to know when uncertainty was impairing his judgment. She realized that Raphael had a good chance of winning this tournament outright. He was that good. Vanessa paid attention to how Raphael moved, his composure, and his stamina. She was building more of that case file in her head. Who was Raphael Johnson?

Raphael spun around at full speed for a powerful chop. His hand moved through the air like a glider while Danny executed a blind sideways kick. A simultaneous smack echoed as Raphael's chop cracked into Danny's back, and Danny's heel hit Raphael's jaw.

Raphael absorbed the hit and continued moving. Danny's back burned and jarred because the chop had done its damage.

Danny regained vision in one eye, with the other watering uncontrollably. Danny started to step backward to escape the losing predicament, and Raphael leaped into the air, orchestrating a spinning back kick. Danny felt the blow to his chest tighten his muscles as he staggered.

Raphael swung his knees through the air in a bicycle motion. Danny felt the force of the knee into the side of his head. It sent Danny stumbling while Raphael repeated the maneuver into Danny's ribcage. A stinging sensation sliced through the area of impact. Some breaths felt like tweezers, and Danny knew another strike like that could break his ribs.

Raphael bent his knee to prepare for the same strike. Danny engaged in another sidekick. Raphael backflipped through the air. Danny's kick flew under its target. Raphael landed on his feet, and Danny charged at him full speed with a swift bicycle kick. His heel snapped into Raphael' sternum.

The crowd lost their breath because they felt how much it hurt. Raphael felt the air suck out of his lungs, and his chest tighten. The pain immobilized him for a split second.

Danny rolled forward. He came out of the roll behind Raphael and wrapped his hands around Raphael' ankles, pulling back. Raphael's stomach smacked against the platform as Danny applied the same ankle lock maneuver from the previous fight. Danny twisted Raphael's ankle with maximum pressure.

Danny let out a war cry that reverberated across the amphitheater.

"Say you quit!" He shouted. "I'll snap it!"

Danny put up a confident front, but on the inside, he was exhausted. His vision was still spotty, and that chop left him with a skin-crawling sensation across his upper body. Danny bent Raphael's ankle further.

"I will never quit!" Raphael screamed, still flat on the ground.

He could have snapped Raphael's ankle right off the bone, but his conscience stopped him. Raphael was a freedom fighter, and he would need to be able to walk to fight. Instead, he applied just enough pressure to make Raphael feel like his ankle was breaking.

Twenty seconds went on while Raphael screamed, his face contorted in pain.

"Say you quit!" Danny demanded

Raphael refused.

Danny's impatience grew, and he knew what he had to do. The same thing he had done to Akira.

A sense of excitement ripped through the amphitheater. Maryse reached out and grabbed Gergio's arm in anticipation, and Vanessa tried to remain focused. This move would signal the end for any ordinary competitor, but Raphael was no ordinary fighter.

Danny prepared to wrap his legs around Raphael to immobilize him. Simultaneously, Raphael placed both hands against the platform and rose to a standing position with his free foot. Danny applied more pressure and came dangerously close to snapping Raphael' ankle.

Raphael kicked his heel backward into Dany's jaw. Danny's mouth was forced shut onto his tongue while Raphael was freed from his grip.

Raphael landed on his back as Danny's arm flailed into the air. Danny tasted the gooey blood dripping from his mouth. Raphael returned to his feet in a kip-up motion and sprinted at Danny.

Raphael lurched into the air, bringing his body sideways and swinging his feet in opposite directions for a scissor kick. The ball of his foot bashed into Danny's pectoral. The pain escaped Danny's mouth with another stagger backward.

Raphael was on his feet again and swung both hands forward in a chopping formation. Danny got his elbows up to protect himself. Raphael switched from his initial attack and snapped a knee into Danny's stomach.

Blood spurted from Danny's mouth. Danny threw his fists up in a boxer formation to protect himself from the next attack, and Raphael was already spinning high through the air for a Jumping Back Kick. He shot his leg backward, and his foot slid in between Danny's fists. More blood spewed from Danny's mouth upon the hit to his jaw. Raphael moved at a speed Danny struggled to follow.

Raphael left his feet again and went for a swift sidekick in midair. The ball of his foot cracked against Danny's forehead. For a split second, Danny's body went numb as unconsciousness tried to break its way in.

Raphael made a third leap into the air in a barrel roll motion. Danny threw himself into Raphael's body to absorb the impact. Raphael's move ended with his waist being constricted by Danny's arms in a bear hug.

Danny squeezed tightly and lifted Raphael into the air. Danny fell onto his back as he sent Raphael's body flipping over him and landing back first onto the ring mat. The impact dulled Raphael's response time with a jarring pain that consumed his entire body.

He lifted Raphael again and snapped him backward just like before. Danny repeated this a third time and snapped even harder. Their comfortable place in the center of the ring was being replaced by the terror of the platform's edge.

Vanessa continued to watch in awe. She could feel the excitement of the crowd growing. Raphael was going toe to toe with Danny. If Danny is throwing him off the platform rather than going for a KO or submission, that means he knows his defeat is hugely possible.

Maryse turned to Georgio, "Tell me. Is it about to be over?"

Georgio did not respond to her. Like the audience, he was locked onto the beauty of the back-and-forth battle.

Danny lifted Raphael up over him once more. He grunted and planted his feet into the ground as he snapped again. Raphael's arms flailed from the speed of the slam, and his back crashed against the platform. The edge of the platform was less than a body length away now.

Danny's arms burned from the strain. His head rocked with each breath.

Danny bent himself over Raphael to lift him again. Suddenly, Raphael wrapped his legs in a triangle form around Danny's neck. Raphael had one foot over the other behind Danny's head to lock in his triangle chokehold. Danny tried to rise up, and Raphael hung from Danny's neck in midair. Their bodies were only a few feet from the platform's edge. Danny's back was facing the edge.

Vanessa sprang to her feet in shock. Danny was so close to the edge that it was now him in danger.

Danny was embarrassed. Raphael took those slams unwillingly and capitalized anyways. Danny wrapped his hands around Raphael's legs to force them off. Raphael lifted his body and wrapped one hand around Danny's head. With his other hand, he chopped at lightning speed.

Danny felt his head reach the stars as he absorbed the chop. His body tilted as he staggered backward. The gap between his body and the edge grew smaller. Raphael lifted his arm up and chopped down again. The impact hurt just as much and put Danny into a panic. His chest was tightening, while his breathing became difficult. His arms were strained from holding Raphael for so long, and the submission hold was on the verge of numbing his body.

His feet crossed over themselves as he stumbled backward. The two feet gap from the edge turned into a foot. The entire audience was glued to the action.

Danny wanted to move, but his legs could not respond. Danny collapsed to one knee with Raphael's back on the platform. Raphael's legs were locked in tighter than ever. Danny's vision sporadically blacked out, with his breathing becoming scarcer. Danny was on the path to unconsciousness.

Danny felt desperation set in as his defeat drew closer.

Raphael sinched his legs around Danny's neck even tighter.

Another memory slipped through Danny's head. It was an echo of his father's words from decades ago, "You keep going! You never give up! You find a way!"

Danny closed his eyes and focused on his breathing. *Find a way. Never give up.*

Danny's adrenaline kicked into overdrive. *Push through! Find a way! Never Give up!* He opened his eyes and grunted. He got both feet under him and stood up. Raphael still had the chokehold locked in, and he hung in mid-air, dangling from Danny's neck.

Danny mustered up the last of his strength and took one step forward, bringing them farther away from the edge. Raphael responded with another chop to the head, and Danny felt the pain all over his body. He took a second step forward and then a third and a fourth

Danny felt for the edge of the platform with his foot and realized he was a safer distance away. Danny grunted as he turned his body clockwise, one step at a time until Raphael' back was now facing the edge. Danny's adrenaline was the only power source keeping him going.

Danny was able to get both hands against Raphael's back and used his grip to lift Raphael further into the air. Danny dove forward and forced his body into free fall with Raphael's legs still wrapped around his neck. Danny's stomach smacked onto the platform while Raphael's body continued to fall to the outside.

Danny's upper body hung over the edge while Raphael's back smacked onto the mat below. Raphael lost grip of his submission upon impact.

The room fell to a sudden silence. Danny's head hung only inches from the floor with his hands planted into the platform's edge. Raphael lay flat on the floor. The seconds seemed like hours as the crowd waited for the referee to make his call. He finally threw his hand into the air with three fingers up.

The gong sounded as Danny's name popped onto the digital board with a "W by DQ" next to it. The crowd responded with excited applause. Audience members talked amongst themselves in amazement at how close the match was.

Danny brought his full body onto the platform and rolled onto his back. He stared at the ceiling lights, fully aware of how easily he could have fallen off the platform with his opponent. The move was a gamble of desperation. The tightness in his chest receded in tiny intervals. His first free breath was like a tidal wave shooting out of his lungs. Feeling returned to his body one part at a time.

Maryse placed her hand over her mouth, "Daniel! No…" she turned to Georgio, "How bad is he hurt?"

Georgio smiled and surveyed the crowd like the only man at a buffet. "I'm sure he's worn out, but do you hear this crowd?! What a battle! The revenue we're going to make on the betting this year…"

Danny crawled to his feet and staggered to the bleachers. A trail of blood streamed from his mouth and dripped off his chin. All the aches and pains his adrenaline suppressed were now loud and proud. He dropped into his seat.

Vanessa handed him the white rag, and he tended to his wounds.

"Very resourceful," Vanessa said, patting him on the back. "How close was it to a double disqualification?"

Danny chuckled in amazement, "Closer than I care to admit. Holy shit. That was too close."

Over the intercom system, the announcer called for a fifteen-minute intermission.

"I'll be back in a second," Danny said. "Gonna run to the locker room for a new rag. You need anything? You good?"

"All good," Vanessa said. "I have to get my head into the game."

Danny was in the locker room digging into his duffle bag. The lighting was dim, and it gave him a moment to calm his brain.

"You are a tremendous fighter."

Danny recognized Raphael's thick Bassakran accent and turned to him. "Thank you. I have a hell of a lot of respect for you too. That was some expert fighting. You know when you had that chokehold in, had you gone for my nose or ribcage with those chops, you probably would have had me."

Raphael sat on a flat bench near Danny, "Excitement of victory got the better of me."

Danny sat a few inches from him and dabbed the fresh rag against his wound. "Happens to us all. You scared the crap outta me."

"I've lived with fear for most of my life," Raphael said. "The Xings never really allowed me to have much else."

Danny made eye contact with Raphael, "If it means anything, I do hate the Xings. I'm sorry."

"So, will you help us?"

Danny dropped the rag and stammered, "I didn't say all that. Brother, now is not a good time for this."

He already knew the answer but was rushing to catch his bearings.

Raphael stared into him.

"You received every message I sent, didn't you?" Raphael asked.

Danny gulped and looked away. His shame was written across his face. Danny stood up and shook his head.

"Please, look at me when I am talking to you," Raphael said.

Danny made eye contact.

"Yes, I did receive them. You got me at a really bad time in my life. That warrior you heard about? He's gone. You get me? He's not here. I've been struggling to find him. I don't say this for your sympathy because I don't dare try to compare my suffering to yours. Just please understand, I've been lost for a long time now. There's been so much pain."

"I do not ask you to pick up a rifle and kill again. I am asking you to simply connect us with the right people to get us the resources we need to overthrow the Xings."

"But you're asking me to take actions that would put rifles in the hands of others that would kill. How is that any different?!"

"Because millions of lives are at stake! Let me remind you, Mr. Richmond, that this is one area that is black and white. The Xings are evil fascists. We're the good guys. We're freedom fighters. We're fighting for liberation."

Raphael paused for a moment to calm himself, "If I had bested you. Would I have earned enough of your respect to get you to change your mind?"

"What?" Danny's jaw dropped. "You have my utmost respect. I mean that. No, it wouldn't have made a damn difference. Whatever your brother made me out to be, I'm not anymore. Okay?"

Raphael sat down on the bench and stared at the ground.

"What is it that you fear?" Raphael asked.

"Remembering everything. Failure. Feeling again. Vincent. The Xings. Fucking everything."

"And there is no way for you to let it go?"

"If there is, I don't know how to. Raphael, I had to teach myself to walk again. For a long time, I felt immortal. I had been shot before, but last time was different. I cheated death."

Raphael put his hand on Danny's shoulder.

"Easy water runs deep," Raphael said.

Danny squinted.

"It's a saying in my country," Raphael said. "We use it to describe people who appear easygoing but deep-down harbor intense emotions within. You are very troubled."

"I'm scarred, man," Danny said bluntly. They shared a warrior's glance in that moment. Raphael finally had a better understanding of what Danny was going through. Raphael carried enough scars for a hundred soldiers. He knew better than to discount the scars Danny was wearing.

"What do you plan to do to heal these scars?" Raphael asked.

"Not back down from my brother's challenge. If I can overcome him, then perhaps I have a shot at bringing myself back to life. It's not that I don't want to help you, Raphael. At this second, I'm literally incapable of it."

"Once this tournament is over, I have something to offer you I know you cannot refuse. Until then, fight with everything you've got. I will be rooting for you."

They shared another warrior's glance. Raphael extended his hand out, and they shook hands.

Raphael had no plans of leaving the country just yet, and Danny knew it. Danny would redirect him to Vanessa if he knew him better. For now, he would keep Vanessa's identity a secret.

Danny made his way to the locker room exit and found Vanessa standing there.

"Vanessa?" Danny asked with a laugh. "You looking for the bathroom?"

Vanessa stared at Raphael, who eventually stared back at her.

"Yea," Vanessa said with a forced laugh. "Clumsy me, getting lost. Where is it?"

Danny pointed her down the hall.

Vanessa thanked him and went about her way. She turned the intersection and then stopped. She peaked around the corner, watching Danny make his way back out to the amphitheater. Minutes passed before Raphael finally came out of the locker room in casual clothing. Vanessa prepared for him to come her way. Instead, he walked back into the amphitheater to continue watching the show.

Well, now's as good of a time as any. She thought. Vanessa did a speed walk into the locker room to Raphael's bag. She went through every piece of it, looking for the hard drive. She stopped for a moment pulling out a laminated photo. It was Raphael with his parents and siblings from a time before the Xings. The smile on Raphael's face was unfamiliar to her. Vanessa remembered reading the report on Raphael's history. He and his sister were the only ones in that photo not killed by the Xings. Not even she was calloused enough to ignore that pain.

Vanessa discovered a sparkly necklace in the duffle bag. In the family photo, Raphael's mother was wearing that same necklace. Vanessa placed the necklace back right where she found it and spent another minute surfing through every nook and cranny of the bag. The hard drive was not there. She made sure everything was neatly back in place, and she zipped the bag back up.

Vanessa kept a mental image of Raphael's family photo in her head. He was still a human being on his own journey. Perhaps his intentions were good, but she couldn't afford to let her guard down yet. Did he have the hard drive on him? She would have to find out later.

CHAPTER THIRTEEN

Intermission was almost over, and Danny sat down next to Vanessa.

"Danny," Vanessa said, "Hope you know you're facing me in the finals. I'm crushing Vincent tonight, and then I defeat you and carry the honor as best fighter in the world."

She smirked, and Danny returned it. She never failed to impress him.

"When you go into this fight," he said, the tone of his voice becoming serious and somber, "don't go putting him on the defensive for too long. Let him come to you. Stick and move, stick and move. I know traditional strategy says to get in close to kill his reach advantage, but if he catches you, it's over. He's got you on size, and he's really got you on strength. What you have is speed, pressure points to attack, and psychological warfare. No woman has ever made a mark in the tournament like you have. That's gotten into the head of everyone, even Vincent."

Vanessa eyed Vincent out of her peripheral vision. He was far enough away to not be able to hear them but not far enough for her guard to be completely down.

The digital board sparked to life. Vanessa Rodes (USA) Vs. Vincent Diezego (USA). The energy in the room exploded with a roar of crowd excitement. Everybody was on their feet. The anticipation for this fight had begun to rival the anticipation for Danny versus Vincent. Vanessa versus Vincent was the impossible fight that could not happen.

Vanessa felt her chest tighten as the seriousness of the fight crystallized in her mind.

"You got this," Danny whispered to her.

They fist-bumped, and Vanessa started her walk to the ring. Danny sighed in worry as he watched her step onto the platform. Vincent soon followed, and they then stood across from each other.

"Georgio," Maryse said. She was trying to remain calm even though she could already feel her heartbeat speed up. "Tell me… Can Vanessa win?"

Georgio again smiled at the crowd's excitement and imagined the money that was sure to follow. "Truth be told, I think Vanessa will win. I bet pretty big on her."

Maryse took a deep breath of relief. She felt Danny was safe with Vanessa. Fighting Vincent terrified her.

Vanessa stood across from Vincent. Her eyes narrowed in on his eyes with the referee's hand in between them.

Vincent smirked, "You know, Vanessa, you really do got a smokin' hot body. Got damn, you're so fine! Why fight each other? Why not just disqualify yourself and have a night out on the town with me? That's a pretty big win if ya' ask the Vin Man!"

Vanessa snorted, "Fuck you, asshole."

Vincent laughed a deep roar of a laugh. His demeanor changed in a moment, and he became deadly serious, "This is your last chance to back out of this fight. I don't want to hurt you. My issues are with Danny boy."

"Then what was Peter? I'm going to make you regret what you've done."

Vincent shrugged, "I had to make a point. You really think you can survive this? I'm serious, Vanessa, I don't want to hurt you. There's no honor in that. Back out now. This is a man's tournament."

Vanessa did not reply because she did not feel she owed him a response. She kept her mind focused. Vincent got into his usual boxer stance while Vanessa got into her stance, shifting back and forth in a continuous motion. This was psychological warfare. Vanessa had to overcome a height, reach, and strength disadvantage. She had the stamina over him, and everybody knew it. She intended to dance around him and tire him out before he could ever lay a hand on her.

The referee looked to Vanessa and then to Vincent.

Vanessa caught the crowd in the corner of her eye and noticed a lot of hung open jaws and smiling faces. She didn't feed off of it. It was no different than grass on a field for her. She began playing out all possible moves in her head.

Her plotting was cut off by the referee's voice and his hand flying into the air. Vanessa's leg rocketed forward like a spear, gliding just under the referee's hand. Her heel cracked into Vincent's jaw, and it caused his head to snap back. She spun around with cat-like speed, her arm swooshing through the air. Her hand chopped hard into the top of Vincent's spine.

Before he could move, she shot her leg forward for a thrust kick. She smacked into his hamstring once and then a second time with the same kick as if she were knocking down a door. She repeated it a third time and followed up with an additional sidekick with the other leg. He spun his body around, and she hopped away, circling around the platform.

"That's right," Danny said, pumping his fist. "Stick and move."

Vincent tried to corral his aggravation. Just as soon as the match started, she had already gotten good hits. He was stronger, but she was strong enough and hit in just the right areas to cause him pain. It irked him and excited him all at once. Vanessa circled around Vincent and slowly closed the gap.

With each shift she took, she seemed to glide through the air like a bird. Vincent found himself spinning in a circle just to keep up with her speed. The gap between them closed inch by inch. One more inch, and she would be within striking distance. Vincent hid his emotions.

She hopped into the danger zone, and he shot his fist forward. Within the blink of an eye, she grabbed his forearm and spun up it like a tornado. She bent her elbow and came around full circle. Her elbow crashed into Vincent's spinal cord. He felt a stinging sensation that caused more mental pain than physical. She unloaded another trio of chop kicks to his hamstring that affected him a little more each time.

She cocked her hand back and swung with an open palm as Vincent turned. The slap across Vincent's face echoed like a shotgun.

The crowd gasped as Vincent screamed. He swung his fist, and she shifted away to safety. The humiliation hurt just as much as the impact.

"How's a slap to the face feel, bitch?!" Vanessa said with a smirk.

Vincent's eyes widened as he stared back at her while the crowd grew louder in excitement.

She began to circle the platform again, "Come on, Vin Man! What's wrong?!" *Stick and move. Stick and move. Don't get cocky.*

Vincent tried not to overthink her strategy. Thinking too much would only make him angry and distract him from the reality of the situation. He honed in on how she seemed to glide through the air. He paid attention to every little detail of her composure.

Vanessa's adrenaline was pumping, and her confidence was growing. She knew that, eventually, he would use his length to take advantage of her strategy. Any strike by Vincent could turn the tides of the battle. She orbited him like a moon circling a planet, but every time she re-entered his atmosphere, she risked attack. She needed to land a blow damaging enough to hurt him without taking a fight-ending strike of her own.

She shot her leg forward for a front kick, and he slipped to the left and countered with his own flying knee attempt. She hopped backward to evade his strike by inches. She winked at him while gliding around the platform. He bit his lip to hide his frustration.

The back-and-forth dance continued for another thirty seconds. Vanessa would move into the danger zone, and Vincent would attack, only for her to hop away untouched.

Vanessa continued to taunt him until Vincent had finally had enough. She feinted a punch high, and when he went to counter with a kick, she Granby rolled past him across the ground and rose to her feet. He spun around to find her open hand smacking him across the face again with another shotgun sound.

The crowd reacted even louder as Vanessa smirked and glided backward. Vincent's fist trembled in rage. The rumble of laughter developing within the crowd only made it sting worse.

Vincent sprinted at her with a war cry of fury. The smacks were intended to throw Vincent off of his game, and it was working. Every attack was designed to wear him down mentally and physically.

"Fucking bitch!" he shouted as he threw his arms out for a tackle.

She leaped into the air with her hands up high. Vincent dove past her, and she executed a midair back kick. Her heel cracked into the back of his neck. Vincent tumbled forward, and his eyes made contact with the outside floor. His heartbeat intensified, realizing his feet were pressed onto the last inch of platform before the edge. The crescendo of her plan was to disorient him until she could kick him to the outside.

She landed on her knees and rolled to her feet. He made quick steps backward and began to turn around. She quickly unloaded with another trio of various kicks to the same hamstring, which weakened it even further. The final hit teetered his body sideways while he struggled to keep his balance.

Vincent straightened himself and then felt another trio of roundhouse kicks hit the same area. Vanessa gave him no time to react as she charged forward like a bull and threw her body into the air for a dropkick. Both her feet snapped into his back. He felt the pain run through his spine, and panic electrify his body as he tumbled toward the edge.

Maryse felt the urge to jump out of her seat in excitement, "Yes! Do it, Vanessa!" she shouted while pumping her fist into the air.

Danny didn't move a muscle with his hand wrapped around his chin. His eyes followed every movement between both fighters. He maintained his best poker face this time. He did not want Vanessa noticing his reaction one way or the other for fear it might impact her judgment.

Vanessa charged at Vincent once more and dove in for a second dropkick, making the crowd's energy grow even stronger. There were exclamations when Vincent spun his body around toward her kick. He wrapped his hands around each other and shot them down like an axe. His fists smashed into her stomach like boulders and sent her body smacking against the platform.

She let out a yelp of pain as she felt the area of impact lock up. Her supporters in the crowd murmured their worry. Danny still remained expressionless.

Vanessa rolled in the opposite direction and kip-upped to her feet. Vincent charged at her while screaming. He took flight and kicked his foot forward. She lurched into the air at greater speeds. His leg grazed her hair while her heel crunched his ribs. His knee cracked against the platform. He placed one hand against the platform while hugging his ribs with the other. Vanessa executed a hook kick that cracked into his temple.

Vincent fell backward and quickly lurched to his feet as Vanessa charged at him. He swung at her with a right hook, and she rolled under it. She came out of the roll gliding into the air with a jumping sidekick into Vincent's back. It cracked into Vincent's spinal cord again. He staggered forward, fighting to stay on his feet.

Through the pain, he swung his forearm around. She ducked the strike and did another open-hand swing. The shotgun sound of the slap was amplified by another symphony of laughter and exclamation from the crowd. She made a posthaste evasion with her usual hopping tactics.

Her handprint was painted red across his face. His disgrace was clear from the expletives he shouted while throwing his arms into the air. The injuries on his body were starting to add up, and his stamina was starting to waver. The pain from every smack lingered with a never-ending sting.

"How fucking dare you!" Vincent screamed at the top of his lungs. "Damn it! What the hell am I doing wrong?! How can somebody be that fast?! It doesn't make any damn sense! I can't even hit her!"

The front row could hear his words, and Vanessa fed off of his aggravation.

Vincent's frustration was starting to boil over. He had three times the strength as Vanessa, but he couldn't utilize it. Every smack to his face was like a switchblade to his pride that filled him with shame. His breathing was getting visibly heavier, along with his body starting to slouch. The constant movement was exhausting him.

Danny took note of Vincent's heavy breathing and the time clock. This was how long Vincent could go before he started to tire out. Vanessa was still running at full speed.

Vanessa made several more strategically placed kicks, hitting him harder each time. The crowd responded frantically. Their screams slowly grew to a roar. They chanted her name as loud as they could.

"Rodes! Rodes! Rodes!" The crowd shouted. Each chant was like a dagger to Vincent's pride.

Vanessa hopped within striking distance and landed a low kick to his ankle. She followed it with another slap to his face. The crowd barely had time to register as Vincent swung his fist like a rocket, and she immediately dropped down to the ground into a side split formation.

She balled her hands into fists and bent her elbows. She shot a powerful uppercut into his testicles and then a second with the other arm. She followed it with a third, a fourth, a fifth, a sixth, and a seventh uppercut. She continued with a few more at maximum strength.

Vincent's face transformed to red as the pitch of his voice rose. He felt the numbing pain run down his legs and around his back. Vanessa jumped to her feet and then into the air, swinging her leg forward. Her shin smacked into his throat at maximum velocity.
Vincent staggered backward, closer and closer to the edge. The pain running through the sensitive areas of his body disabled him from any

quick motion. Vanessa moved in with a swift volley of kicks and strikes.

Vanessa snapped her leg forward for a thrust kick into Vincent's solar plexus. A wave of nausea and severe pain forced Vincent into a bent-over position. She twirled her other leg through the air and connected with a crescent kick to his head. She continued with her assault of strikes focusing on his throat and legs to keep him weakened. Each strike sent him back a few inches more.

A smile grew on her face. *One more powerful kick, and he's off the platform!*

The honor of being the best fighter of all was drawing closer. She was going to save Danny too. She connected with a knee to his temple and then a straight kick to his solar plexus again, then a hammer kick to his shin, and then another straight punch to his throat.

Vincent's body was only centimeters from the edge, and Vanessa leaped into the air to execute a spinning heel kick. Like a helicopter blade, she swung around full circle.

She felt the enormous weight of Vincent's hands wrap around her shin. Vincent rocketed his elbow down, and it crashed into her ankle like an avalanche of boulders. She felt an explosive pain run through the area of impact while she collapsed onto the platform.

The pain rocked her very senses, but she forced through it and rolled away. With her hands against the platform, she executed a kip-up to her feet. Upon landing, she felt the lightning bolt of pain shoot through her ankle.

She tilted sideways in agony and began to hop backward, but the pain quickly became unbearable. Each piece of her ankle felt like a bed of nails were twisting the bone and digging into it.

Vincent twirled his head around to walk off the pain of her hits. They had been strong enough to wound him but not enough to end him.

Vincent walked up to Vanessa in his boxer stance, and she executed a lightning-quick roundhouse kick to the body. Her body came down on her ankle and her kick limped to a halt as she fought to keep her balance.

Vincent remembered every slap she had landed. He zipped his heel forward and smashed it into her solar plexus. Her body bent forward, and she felt gusts of air escape her mouth. Her stomach tightened into knots as she limped backward, trying to hold back the dry heaves forcing their way out of her mouth.

Vanessa's eyes began to water. *No! No! Damn it!*

"Vanessa," Vincent said, shaking his head. "Give up. Your ankle's wrecked, and you've lost your speed... You've been defeated."

Vanessa's panic took control, and there was nothing she could do to hide the terror in her face. He was right, and she knew it.

"I've come this far," she said, forcing a smile. "I'm going to be the best fighter, you son of a bitch!"

Vanessa had carried the guilt of Danny's accident with her for so long, which compounded with her current humiliation. First, her best friend gets shot on her watch, and now this?

Maryse looked back and forth between them in horror at the turn of the tides.

Danny closed his eyes for a moment in frustration. *She needs to give up. It's over. He's won.*

Vanessa moved in closer to Vincent in her fighting stance without shifting. She limped toward him, step by step.

He shook his head once again while getting into his fighting stance, "Why? Vanessa, you're being foolish... Feel stupid about those slaps, I bet. Look, you lost. Just back away."

"Fuck you!" she shouted as she kicked faster than the blink of an eye.

She used her healthy foot as her base and sent her other shin cracking into Vincent's side. Vincent's body jerked while her shin screamed in agony. A yelp of pain escaped her mouth, and she nearly collapsed.

Vincent clenched his fist tightly, bent his elbow, and pulled his arm back. He waited for only a second and then exploded with a straight punch that smashed into her chest. Like Peter, she felt an extreme tightness form. Her breathing went from rapid gasps to panicked wheezing. The tightness turned into a tweezer-like pain that grew sharper.

Vincent stood still, "This is pointless. I don't want to hurt you any longer. Give up."

Vanessa ignored all logic and refused to quit. She engaged in a right hook, and Vincent grabbed her forearm. He executed another boulder-like punch, smashing into her shoulder and dislocating it. It was another sign of the inevitable. He released her arm.

"Give up!" He shouted.

Many in the crowd flinched in their seats from the sound of the hit.

Her arm dangled lifeless, swinging back and forth while drooping down. The injury sent a chill through her veins. She had completely forgotten about her official mission. Her ego and her will to protect Danny had completely blinded her. Vincent was her tunnel vision.

She refused to give up. She had to be the champion. She kept that thought at the forefront of her brain. Victory was within her grasp, and she fell victim to overzealousness like she had so many times before.

Danny leaped from the bleacher and shouted, "Vanessa, take your own advice to Peter and submit! For your own good!"

Maryse was speechless. Her hopes of saving Danny were gone, and the gruesome nature of the tournament was once again displayed to her. She turned to Georgio, and he shared the same look of horror as the rest of the audience.

Vanessa had a million thoughts running through her mind. She plotted a way to victory. If she could just goad him to the edge of the platform, she could still trip him off. Maybe she could get in a powerful kick to the head and knock him out, right? The possibilities were endless and clever tactics of denial.

Vanessa attempted a combination of punches. Vincent deflected each one and responded with another series of punches that left her on the ground. The crowd reacted with each hit.

Vincent screamed to the referee, "Call the match! It's over!"

Danny's eyes were watery, "Vanessa, stay down, damn it! It's over!"

The referee rushed over to Vanessa and kneeled down to check on her. She lay unresponsive as the referee went to signal a knockout victory. He started to get his arm into the air, and Vanessa placed an elbow against the platform. The referee stopped while she crawled to her feet. Her body was aching. Her eyes were filled with watery tears of regret. She fought to stay conscious as the room around her spun out of control.

"Damn it, Vanessa!" Danny shouted from the bleachers. "Let it go! Vincent, you son of a bitch, just toss her out! You made your point!"

Vincent walked behind her. He wrapped his forearm around her arms to hold her in place and dragged her to the edge of the platform.

"This is pathetic," Vincent said.

Vanessa freed her arm and elbowed him, but her strength was gone. He simply took the impact and trapped her arms again. The noise of the audience became a nuisance to Vanessa. The colorful lights of the amphitheater felt like a spotlight on her humiliation.

Vincent paused and stared at Danny. A smirk grew on his face. He had her at the edge and simply let go. For Danny, it all happened in slow motion. Her body tumbled off the platform and to the mat below.

Danny sprinted to Vanessa and kneeled down next to her. Paramedics rushed in, and he backed away. He stood up and made eye contact with Vincent. The gong of victory went off, but it was not met with fanfare. Most of the crowd was silent in shock. Danny and Vincent stood in emotional turmoil. Rage had so consumed Danny that it obscured the foundation of fear underneath it.

Vincent let out a quick laugh that was interrupted by his heavy breathing, "Don't you fuckin' look at me like that. I gave her a million opportunities to give up... She did this to herself!"

Danny noticed Vincent's chest heaving from exhaustion. He made note of the match's length by taking a split-second look at the digital board. *This is how long I have to last to beat him, but can I?*

CHAPTER FOURTEEN

Nighttime was relaxing for most people. Danny often hated the loneliness he found in the night. Years of CIA work made the situation unbearable. The endless sounds of gunfire and the faces of his targets were inescapable. He lay in bed with his thoughts on Vincent. It was as if their entire past together was happening all at once. Maryse was asleep next to him, but it did little to comfort him.

His mind kept coming back to the same image: Vincent's smirk just before tossing Vanessa off the platform.

He tapped his cranium into the headboard a few times and sighed. He observed the strips of moonlight painted over his bed. Even with Maryse by his side, he was alone.

He watched Vanessa's body collapse to the ground over and over again. His heart was in turmoil. He was enraged over what Vincent had done to Vanessa and Peter. But he was also resentful toward Vincent for what he had done to him. Under his turmoil was his desire to have his best friend again. He knew the old Vincent still had to be in there somewhere.

His conflict was interrupted by Maryse turning to face him. Danny looked her in the eyes, and she returned it. He could tell she had not been asleep, but that she had been crying.

Danny looked away, not able to hold her gaze. He looked instead at the moonlight running across his bed as he tried to gather his thoughts. He turned to her again, unable to speak.

"Just spit it out," she said to break through the barrier. "You know this will not end until we talk about it."

"Maryse," Danny said. "I have to do this. I hope you understand why. I know it ain't makin' much sense."

"You have to do it?" Maryse massaged her temples, and her voice became a whisper. "Are you crazy?!"

"No. I'm not crazy," Danny said, objecting to the word. "I'm a fighter. Vincent was my blood brother... You couldn't understand. We saved each other's lives so many times in the past."

"So, he was your brother, and now you seek to destroy each other," Maryse said, sitting up and crossing her arms. Her voice was quiet no longer. "Is it that simple? Does your brutality really come down to such primitiveness?"

"Yea, it's that simple," Danny said, raising his voice in kind. Spite curdled the edges of his words. "He hurt me, and to be honest with ya', it hasn't stopped hurtin'. I just have to know if I can still go. I walked away from everything I once knew two years ago. After our last fight, I ran from the tournament. I ran from the torn bonds between us. I don't expect my words to be makin' sense, but I just hope you understand there is no other way."

She threw her arms out, "Understand what? That you want to fight a man who wants to cripple you? And why? So, you can be best fighter of all?! If you do not understand the downright insanity in your logic, then I am confused at how you have made it so far in life. Why not be best in something healthy? Like a therapist or a schoolteacher? Why must you be the best at breaking peoples' bones?!"

"It's about the honor."

"Oh, do not lecture me about honor! It is about toxic masculinity. Ego. Miss Rodes suffers from it too. Miss Rodes just had to fight, and where did it leave her? How about your friend Peter? Where did it leave him? Both of them are in the hospital!"

"Hey, Vanessa will be okay. Doctors simply had to pop her shoulder back into place. Her ankle is just bruised, not broken. She'll make a full recovery."

Her voice raised to an echo, "Oh, and that makes it safe then, Daniel?! So, she will only be in crutches and in a sling for a month, so everything is okay?! This is madness."

He shrugged and raised his voice a little, "Maybe it is, but it ain't changin' my course of action. If you can't bear to watch it, then don't come. I know I sound like a cold-hearted asshole, but it really comes down to bein' that simple."

She placed her head into her hands and ran them through her hair. She turned her head away and let her mind do the mental work. It was a life she would never understand. If she had the power, she would shut the entire tournament down and have Georgio arrested for putting it together.

She turned to him, "Your heart is set on this brutal showdown..."

He nodded, "Yes. I can't be backin' down now. Not after comin' this far. There's much about my past you don't know. I walk around with a lot of scars, a lot of regret. Not a day has gone by where I haven't thought about Vincent. To this day, I will play out an alternate scenario in my head where we worked things out. Where he, Selena, and I continued on our missions saving the world. Call me obsessive, fine, I will take it. But the obsession needs to end. Because of equal value to all the regret is the embarrassment of our last fight. I was set to let it burn away in the past, and then he challenged me again. At a time when I have stepped away from the life I once felt destined for. If I'm ever going to be able to stand up for the free world again, I need to know I am still Dragon Heart."

Maryse placed her hand on his cheek and moved in for a slow kiss. They exchanged it only for a second. She spoke a soft line in French and then said in English, "Daniel, may God be with you in this fight. I will be there to watch and cheer you on. I do not condone this fighting, but I realize there is no changing your mind. Just do me a favor?"

"Anything, Maryse..."

"Win."

He was unsure if she wanted him to respond, but he did not. The truth of the matter was he couldn't promise her anything. Peter's fighting career was over for good, and perhaps his wrestling career as well, and Vanessa was in a hospital bed. The moment of truth was approaching. Danny Richmond was going to face the greatest challenges he had ever come to know. His brother and his fears.

Danny was shirtless and alone in the bathroom, staring at his reflection in the mirror. The final memories of his last fight with Vincent pushed their way through.

Vincent looked at Danny the same way he did an enemy on a mission. Danny had two options, continue the fight and risk being further beaten to a pulp by Vincent, or give in to how easy it would be to just fall off the platform. The former would be dangerous for his long-term health. The latter guaranteed his ability to recover physically while mentally leaving him to endure the shame and embarrassment of disqualifying himself from the fight.

Each step Vincent took toward Danny was a second less Danny would have the use of his legs. Danny refused to ever say the words 'I quit' and closed his eyes. Danny fought to ignore his injuries. Vincent was taken by surprise as Danny shot his legs into the air in a bicycle formation. Danny's connected into Vincent's nose, snapping it and leaving red painted across his face.

Danny tried to lift his leg for another attack, but the blood in his throat robbed him of air and caged his movements. Danny coughed the blood out of his mouth rather than moving. Vincent blindly rocketed his forearm, and it slammed into Danny's forehead. Danny's vision blurred in a repeat pattern while he stumbled backward. His one foot pressed against the platform while the other found nothing but air outside the platform. Gravity began to pull his body and Danny had to make a choice on what he would do.

Vincent was able to clear his vision. His triumph was quickly replaced by horror, watching Danny's body falling off the platform. In one second, Vincent threw his arms out to grab him, and in the next, it was over.

Danny's back hit the floor. He felt humiliated and betrayed by both himself and Vincent. The crowd all stood up in dead silence while the final gong was rung. Vincent stared up at the digital readout, "Winner: Vincent by Disqualification."

Vincent stared at Danny's bloody body on the floor with his own wave of humiliation and rage. The crowd chatter was all on one issue. Danny was never KO'd or submitted. He simply lost his balance and fell off the platform. Was this a fluke? It ate Vincent alive.

Lying on his back and staring at Vincent's crimson mask, Danny knew the truth. He chose the easy way out by throwing himself off the platform. Danny had submitted, but neither Vincent nor the world would ever know it.

Danny opened up his eyes to his own reflection in the mirror. The truth gnawed away at his pride, cutting a knife through his dignity.

CHAPTER FIFTEEN

Sleep had eluded Danny Richmond. He dreaded the soon-to-be-rising sun, and the day it would bring. Danny sat on his front lawn with his mind on Vincent's dismantling of Vanessa and Peter. He looked up at the sky turning purple as morning came.

How am I going to defeat him? He thought to himself. Tomorrow was the fight, and it was all he could think about it.

The headlights of a vehicle swept across his driveway. He recognized Vanessa's sports car immediately. She rolled down the passenger window.

"Get in," she said bluntly.

Danny protested and expected a back-and-forth squabble. The back window rolled down and to his surprise Peter poked his bruised head out.

"Danny. Just listen to her."

Danny got into the passenger's seat. He took a quick note of their health. Vanessa was in an arm sling and ankle brace. She wore the bruises of her fight all over her body. Peter's arm was casted tightly in place, with the bruises of his fight fading away from his face.

Soon enough, their vehicle was headed south on the Illinois 294 expressway.

"Anybody want to tell me where the hell we're headed?" Danny said with his hand to his head. "This is crazy."

The car was silent. The sounds of other cars rumbled all around them.

"Good talk." Danny rolled his eyes.

Danny saw the sign. Dempster St. Route 14. Next Two Exits.

"Wait." Danny's heart began to beat faster. "Where the fuck are we going?"

Des Plaines, Illinois had always felt like home to him. There was only one place they could be taking him. Ten minutes went by, and they pulled into a driveway. The two-story house's age was masked by the lush garden dominating the front lawn. The morning dew glistened off every piece of foliage.

"You guys realize it's 6:30 in the morning, right?" Danny asked.

"Yea?" Vanessa smiled. "You realize I already texted her, right? She's been awake for a while now. Come on, we're going in."

By the time they closed the car doors behind them, the front door of the house had already been opened. Judith Richmond stood with a smile brighter than the sun. Her features reflected her six decades on the planet.

"My God." Judith's jaw dropped as she looked at their injuries. "Don't tell me you guys let Danny talk you into fighting with him in that god-awful tournament?"

"What? Mom. No." Danny threw his arms into the air. "I didn't ask them to do anything."

Judith looked at him with the type of investigative eyes that only mothers could utilize. Danny had remembered a moment similar to this when he and Vincent had come home late as teenagers. Apparently, some things never change.

"Come inside, all of you. Breakfast is already set up." Judith said.

She hugged all of them as they hobbled into the house. Judith hugged Danny a little longer and expressed her motherly affection for him.

Vanessa and Peter walked further into the house, leaving Danny with his mom, who locked the door behind her. Danny had every intention to hide how he was really feeling on the inside. The few bruises he carried from his fights were nothing compared to the atomic bomb that detonated within his soul.

"You look worse than they do," Judith said.

"I'm fine, Mom."

"No, you're not. Talk to me. You're just like your father when you're troubled." Judith could see behind his poker face. No amount of training ever gave him the skills to fool his mother.

Minutes later, Danny was sitting in the family room with Judith.

Danny had his hands folded together, and he leaned forward. He was shaking his head and laughing.

"I really do miss you," he said. "How you been, Ma?"

"If you answered my calls more, you'd know. I'm well. It's you I'm worried about."

He shrugged off her concerns.

"When you gonna ask Vanessa to marry you?"

"What?!" He sat upright.

"Oh, come on!" Judith brushed him away. "Don't play dumb with me. I see the way you two look at each other. It's always been that way."

"I'm in a committed—"

"With that model? What's her name? When you gonna' introduce her to me?" Judith cut him off. "Give me a break. Your grandma, God rest her soul, would be calling you an idiota with her thick Italian if she were here now. That model girl is just a rebound. Vanessa's the real keeper. She's been here for ya' during the best and worst."

They went on a little longer about Vanessa. Danny shared things he loved about Vanessa and the positive influence she had on his life. He talked about her resolve, intelligence, and passionate personality. Judith could not understand why Danny was not with her.

Their lighthearted conversion turned to Vincent, and Danny's smile disappeared.

"I love both of my sons." Judith shook her head. "It hurts me to see you two fighting like this."

"I didn't start this, Ma. He did." Danny said.

"You didn't start this, but don't forget he's still your brother. He needs help. He needs to come home."

"You've been keeping in touch with him?" Danny asked.

"When he actually answers his phone, yea. You know, I've always hated this martial arts and CIA stuff. It killed me whenever your father would go away on assignment. I'm glad you're outta that dangerous business. I wish you'd just leave the fighting behind you too."

Danny thought it was best to not tell her that Vanessa's been trying to recruit him back into the service. Danny and Judith talked for a little while longer about his own mental state. It calmed Danny to hear her wise words. Judith always had a way of getting him to open up in ways that no one else ever could. Danny talked to her about almost anything, and she usually had a calming answer for him.

Danny spent the next few minutes opening up to her a little more about how he was feeling, and she hugged him as tightly as she could.

Vanessa and Peter stood in the family room looking at a glass case stuffed with trophies, medals, and photos. Most of them were of Danny and Vincent from all different stages of their lives.

Vanessa took notice of a photo of Danny and Vincent sitting next to each other in kindergarten. They were laughing so hard their eyes were closed, and Vanessa wondered what it could have been about. She observed another photo from their teenage years, one where the boys were training with Thomas Richmond. A third photo was of them with Judith and Thomas. Danny and Vincent were both in their military blues, having just graduated boot camp with the Marine Corps. Another was of Danny and Vincent being awarded the Distinguished Intelligence Cross, the highest decoration awarded by the CIA. The actual medals sat in plaques just below the photo.

"Holy shit," Vanessa muttered. Her eyes became watery as she bit her tongue. The deep connection of their bond showed in every photo. The history of Danny and Vincent had never been this clear to her before. Danny had stopped speaking about Vincent a few years back. It usually took hard liquor to get him to open up about the situation.

"Fun fact," Peter said. "I was there the day Judith took that photo of the three of them training. It was one of the craziest things I'd ever seen as a teenager."

"What happened to Vincent's parents?" Vanessa asked.

"Danny's parents raised Vincent as their own. Vincent's biological dad was an abusive alcoholic, and I never understood his mom. I don't know what's happened to them now," Peter said.

"Alright, are any of you kids going to tell me what the hell happened?" Judith broke their concentration.

Peter and Vanessa gave her a quick rundown of how everything came to be. Judith simply shook her head and brushed her hair back.

"You know," Judith said. "I always hated this martial arts stuff. Their profession too. It's genetical with them, though. Tom learned it from his father, who learned it from Tom's grandfather."

Judith paused herself. The regret and frustration were plain to see. She simply smiled as if to bury it all again, "Come on. Let's eat, everyone."

They all walked into the kitchen. The homemade spread of scrambled eggs, sausage, French toast, pancakes, and other breakfast foods excited them. The kitchen still carried the heat from all of the cooking. Every problem they faced had suddenly disappeared. Judith went to the music device on the kitchen counter and turned on a playlist of classic feel-good songs from their childhood.

"Mrs. Richmond!" Peter shouted. "I have missed your cooking!"

Peter shared with Vanessa how often he would come over on the weekends for these meals. Before long, they were all seated and digging in, laughing as each story was shared.

Vanessa listened intently as Judith shared funny stories of Danny and Peter from their childhood. She threw in funny stories of Vincent in a way that did not feel threatening or bring down the mood. Danny playfully cringed at every embarrassing story. The minutes turned into an hour as the good times rolled on. The music flowed from one song to the next in a perfect set.

Vanessa wanted to know every detail. She was greedy for every anecdote about their childhood antics, and Judith was more than willing to provide them. They all shared a lot of laughs and jokes along the way.

"I stand by that jacket! It was cool!" Danny shouted with a laugh.

"You wore it everywhere," Judith reinforced.

"He wanted to wear it to Prom," Peter said.

Danny tried to defend himself, but when Judith pulled out an old photo album, Danny's case was lost. They went through a large portion of the photo album. Eventually, Judith brought out Danish pastries, and they continued to swap stories. Peter and Vanessa surfed through every page of the photo album. Vincent was in there just as much as Danny.

Danny, Peter, and Vanessa were on the back porch of Judith's home. The sounds of Des Plaines traffic reverberated in the distance. There was a warm breeze that ran against their bodies, with the tree leaves swaying in the wind.

Vanessa was seated in a chair, "I want to apologize, Danny."

"For what?" Danny asked. He was standing and leaning against the patio railing.

"Looking through all those photos of you and Vincent. The medals. The stories from your mom. I get it now. How close you two were. I get why you have to fight. This isn't about ego or revenge. He's your mirror image, and if you can't beat and rescue him, then how can you overcome your own demons?"

"Thank you," Danny said. "Vincent's my brother. I love him. He's also my biggest—" Danny hesitated. "Fear. Truth is, I'm scared to go into this fight. I'm scared of him. I'm scared of what happened to you guys, happening to me."

Danny took another pause to let his words soak in and continued after a deep breath, "Vincent's a part of my history. I ran away from Vincent a decade ago. You all know what happened last time. I threw myself off to save myself. I submitted without ever saying the words. If I don't stand up to him now, if I don't try to rescue him, then how am I ever going to be able to stand up to myself?"

"You're not gonna make our mistakes," Peter said. "I underestimated him. I tried to beat him at his game. That got me crushed."

"I got overzealous," Vanessa said. "My classic self. I went in for the kill too soon. It cost me the match."

"I won't underestimate him, and I know my limitations. So, then what the fuck do I do?" Danny asked.

For dramatic effect, Vanessa carefully rose to her feet, "You let it all go. You stop running from your past and just face it. I know I kept talking about you not being able to fight him, but I was wrong to do that. Deep down, have you ever actually felt you could beat him?"

"I don't know," Danny shrugged. "All I knew was that I had to face my fears. To be honest, it's always been a little bit of a suicide mission, I guess. A desperate gamble."

"Then you need to consider that you can actually win. You always were able to beat him before. How?" Vanessa asked.

"I don't remember every little detail anymore," Danny said with a frown. "I do remember outlasting him and outsmarting him. That was the key every time. I just don't remember exactly how. That part is scary too."

"Then fuck the fear!" Vanessa shouted while Peter pumped his fist in agreement. "Danny, remember, you've got the fire of a dragon running through your fuckin' veins! When death has smiled at you, you've smiled right back. Bring out that Danny Richmond. Bring out the loudmouthed badass motherfuckin' warrior who doesn't take shit from anybody!"

Danny stared into her eyes. Her passion flowed through with every word. She spoke with her finger in the air, and her voice grew louder.

"Since when the fuck do you fear anybody?!" Vanessa continued. "You've literally given dictators the middle finger. You've spat in the faces and whooped the asses of some of the evilest people on this damn planet. You've raised hell all over the world. Remember every mission, every martial arts fight, and every single-fucking-moment you stood your ground. Remember every time you stood up for the vulnerable without hesitation."

Danny soaked in everything she said. His heartbeat picked up with every passing second. He was still speechless as Vanessa went on.

"I'm echoing what Vanessa's saying," Peter said. "Remember when you kicked the shit out of my bullies in high school? You're a fuckin' Marine. You tell fear to go straight to hell. It's time to do that with Vincent. Vincent's human, he's not a monster. He's got limitations and weaknesses. Vanessa and I failed to overcome them, but that doesn't mean you'll fail too. You got into this thing to find the original you. What would the original you do in this situation?"

Danny looked at them both and stood up straight, "He'd get his ass together, develop a strategy, and use it to win. He'd go in with pragmatic courage and logic. He'd refuse to be intimidated."

"Then don't let Vincent intimidate you," Vanessa said.

Danny nodded. They all knew it was easier said than done.

"I love you guys. Honestly, I do. Thank you," Danny said to them both. "Just promise me you'll both be there tomorrow."

"We will," they said in unison.

The three of them hobbled in for a group hug. Danny did not know what tomorrow would bring. He did not know if he would be humiliated or victorious. All he knew was that he had to stand up to Vincent, and more importantly, he had to stand up to himself.

CHAPTER SIXTEEN

Vanessa hobbled with each step she took and used a crutch to keep pressure off her ankle.

Her pride still ached, and she mourned the fact that she was now going to be experiencing the finals from the front row rather than the platform. She stopped in front of Georgio, who had an open seat next to him.

"Do you need any help?" he asked, rising cordially.

"I should be fine, thank you," she said as she slowly sat down while placing the crutch on the floor next to her.

"I am sorry for the damage you took," he said, noticing the swelling over her eye and the sling on her arm. The evidence of her battle with Vincent was written all over her body. A pang of guilt struck him as he thought about the exciting amount of money he had made from the fight. "I hope you are alright."

"My pride hurts more than the physical pains," she admitted. "Doctors say I will make a full recovery."

Maryse sat in the chair on the other side of Georgio. Her eyes were locked on her phone.

"Hopefully, Danny can pull it off," Vanessa said to Maryse, offering her what she thought was an olive branch.

"You failed," Maryse said without looking up from her phone. "I really have no use for you now."

"You're lucky you're Danny's girl," Vanessa said, turning her eyes toward the platform, "or I'd knock your teeth down your throat."

"Ladies," Georgio said, puffing up his chest and trying to intercede in this conflict. "Let's try to remain focused on the contest. Please."

Vanessa looked around the amphitheater at the crowd of people. Every single one of them held pieces of betting paper in their hands. Their eyes were wide with glee, and they spoke in fast-paced conversations with their compatriots. She took only a moment to look for any suspicious characters. The fight with Vincent had stolen some of the concentration from her mission. She saw Raphael sitting only five people down from her in the front row. Peter was seated next to Georgio.

"What are the betters saying about this one?" Vanessa asked Georgio.

"This match, Danny versus Vincent, has already hit record high. Crowd is pretty much split fifty-fifty."

"Do you think Danny can win?" Vanessa asked.

Georgio shrugged, "I didn't think you would lose."

It was not the answer she wanted to hear.

Yoshi Toroko stood at his table and spoke into a microphone, "Thank you all for being here for the final bout. Through the week, we have seen the best fighters from all over the globe give you their heart, body, and soul, all for the honor of being the Golden Dragon champion. With that honor comes the label of being number one. It is not an attribute to be taken lightly. As we continue into our third decade of the tournament, I want to send out my personal gratitude to every fighter who has made this the spectacle of art it has become. We started off with many, and now we are down to two. Tonight, Danny Richmond and Vincent Diezego, you will be cementing your spot into eternity. It is now time for the main event!"

The crowd responded with a standing ovation.

Danny Richmond made a slow-paced walk up the steps of the platform. He ran through every memory he could of Vincent. He could feel his heart rate increase and his mouth get dry. He had not had this feeling in years, not since his first tournament. He struggled to keep his breathing regular. It took focus to keep his hand from trembling.

Danny's mind replayed the other times he stepped onto the platform to face Vincent. He remembered the strength and confidence he felt in those days. Standing on that platform, his former sense of assurance was all but a memory.

Vincent walked up the steps of the platform. The sight of him forced Danny to confront the rage and fear boiling inside him like a pot of water about to overflow. Vincent appeared to be confident and strong in his demeanor. The usual smile that was plastered on his face before fights was absent. He kept his poker face on, which left Danny and the audience to wonder what was going on inside of him.

Danny and Vincent stood only a few feet away from each other. Neither of them could muster the strength to speak. Vincent was the nightmare come to life for Danny. The last battle they had ended in controversy for the fans. Yet, for Danny, there was no controversy.

Vincent stood across from Danny, embroiled in his own rage. Their last encounter left him more humiliated than before. Danny had fallen off the platform, which robbed him of the honor of forcing Danny into submission or knockout. In the eyes of the fans, his victory would always have the asterisk next to it. They believed he beat Danny only by a technicality. That ate Vincent alive almost every day of his life. For Vincent, Danny had become the villain who betrayed him and then mocked him in battle. He could not find peace until he proved to himself that he was capable of besting Danny in battle.

Maryse tapped Vanessa's shoulder, "Miss Rodes?"

"Yes, Maryse?" Vanessa asked, perplexed.

"Can Daniel win? You have great fighting expertise. I must know."

Vanessa instantly thought of Georgio's response to her when she had asked the same question and how it annoyed her. In the face of the same question, she could think of no better response. "I didn't think I'd lose."

She was confused by Maryse suddenly treating her with respect. Vanessa turned back to observe Danny and Vincent.

"I can answer that question," a man sitting on the other side of her said.

Maryse looked over at Vanessa and Georgio, but they were whispering to one another. They didn't seem to have noticed the man seated to her left. For reasons she could not understand, she felt the need to talk with him, "You can?"

"Sure. See that look on Danny's face right now? That is not the Dragon Heart going in there. That is the look of a man fighting in fear and anger. If Danny goes into his fight with Vincent like this, he won't win. But, if he can find himself again, if he can unleash the Dragon Heart, he'll be able to pull it off. I have a feeling Dragon Heart will come back tonight. You just watch."

Maryse leaned back, "And who are you?"

"Oh, I am sorry. Where are my manners? I'm Thomas Richmond. I'm Danny's father."

Maryse's jaw dropped. From his facial structure to the style of his hair, there was no denying the resemblance. His appearance was that of Danny, twenty years older, with some wrinkles and grey hair.

She still found it hard to believe, and he could sense it. Thomas reached into his pocket and pulled out his wallet. He held out a picture of him standing behind a fourteen-year-old Danny and Vincent.

"I trained both of them," he said, putting the picture away. "They're my sons. They both turned out to be tremendous fighters."

Maryse thought of telling Vanessa, but something compelled her not to.

The referee looked back and forth from Danny to Vincent. He hesitated to start the match. Even with all his years of officiating, this year brought brutality beyond most others. He also remembered officiating the last Danny versus Vincent fight. The entire audience shared the feelings of suspense, hesitation, and excitement, all mixed into one.

Danny tried everything he could to focus in on his breathing and anything else to relax his mind. Nothing worked. Vanessa and Peter were physically broken, and they were in the front row as a constant reminder of what Vincent had done to them. No different than what Vincent had done to him in the past.

Vincent tasted a small sense of satisfaction, finally getting the opportunity to rectify what had been a decade-long nightmare for him. Where Danny was full of rage and fear, Vincent was full of rage and confidence.

The referee took one last look at them both and then threw his hand into the air.

The fight had finally begun, and Danny did not hesitate. He whipped his leg forward, and his heel cracked into Vincent's chest. Vincent's body jerked backward, and Danny leaped into the air, spinning. His heel came around full force and clocked Vincent in the head, forcing his body to arch forward.

Danny took the opportunity of a prone opponent to throw a flying knee toward Vincent's chest, hoping to end the match quickly. Vincent threw his hands up, but Danny's strike broke the defense, and his knee connected with Vincent's chest. Vincent staggered backward while his arms flung into the air.

Danny sprinted toward Vincent and rolled forward. He lurched out of the roll with his fist headed for Vincent's jaw. A thud echoed on impact as Vincent staggered again. Each step backward brought Vincent closer to the edge of the platform.

Danny felt those two familiar emotions, fear and rage. He knew he had to end Vincent quickly because he did not believe in himself to be able to go the distance.

Vanessa kept her reactions silent and watched the action intently. She showed neither excitement nor worry.

Danny executed a straight punch into Vincent's chest. Once again, Vincent was sent backward. The edge of the platform was only two feet away. Danny could feel the taste of victory on his lips. It was sour. His fighting spirit wanted the knockout or submission victory, but his fear wanted to end it with his bones intact.

Danny shot a thrust kick to Vincent's solar plexus, and Vincent's arms once again flailed helplessly as he staggered. The edge was now mere inches away.

Danny felt a rush of anxiety run through him. All he had to do was close the gap between him and Vincent. He had to finish it now. The crowd would be disappointed at the length of the match, and he would be stuck with the asterisk victory in his mind. The spectators would say he played the smart game and won it early. The fans would say he robbed them of a good match but did what he had to do. He would know he ran from the fight again, and it would eat him alive.

Danny sprinted forward and lurched into the air. He shot his leg forward like a spear. He came rocketing toward Vincent and felt the calmness of safety start to run through him. This was going to be over, and his enemy would be vanquished. Vincent snapped his leg into the air, and his heel smashed into Danny's chest.

The crowd gasped at the impact.

Danny's body collapsed against the platform. A physical pain shot through the area of impact, and a mental pain far greater consumed his mind.

Danny rolled away and did a kip-up to his feet. He returned to his fighter stance as he took a few steps back. Vincent cleared the edge and put himself in a safe place on the platform.

Vincent got into his boxer stance and smiled, "Oh come on, Danny boy, did ya' really think the Vin Man would die just like that?"

Danny said nothing and hoped his poker face was as strong as he was trying to make it.

Vincent continued, "How many times must I say it? Vincent Diezego does not die! He lives on forever!"

Danny and Vincent began to circle the platform. Vincent took small steps toward Danny, spiraling toward him like a wolf circling its prey. He was not in striking distance, but the feints he used to edge closer were enough to agitate Danny's nerves.

"Ya smell that, Danny?" Vincent said, sniffing the air theatrically. "It's fear... I smell it real good. You reek of it. Can you believe it's come down to this? The great Danny Richmond! The Dragon Heart? Or does anyone still call you that? Is it Mr. Brain Damage now? All of that money and all of those luxuries have made you soft, and now you are face-to-face with the man who is going to cripple you."

Danny wiped a bead of sweat from his forehead, but just as quickly, it was replaced with another. He was taking deep breaths already, his mouth hung open. Vincent chuckled, and it was loud enough for the front row to hear him.

"You're already sweating. Oh, come on, you can't even talk back? The fuck is wrong with you? Don't you find this exciting?! Brother versus brother!"

"I get it," Vincent continued, still smirking at Danny, licking his chops as he continued to circle. "You're frustrated. Your plan was to end me in under a minute. You wanted to blitz me, knock me off the platform. And it failed. Damn, do I love seeing that look of terror in your face!"

Vincent stepped another inch closer to Danny. Danny flinched as if Vincent had made a full-blown assault. The smile on Vincent's face enraged him.

Vincent continued, "I'm going to fuckin' humiliate you just like you did me for so many years. The golden boy is finally going to get the ass kickin' he's deserved for a long while. How does that fear taste? Can't say I know it."

Danny bit his lip and realized his poker face was not working. Vincent inched another step closer.

"Fuck you, Vincent!" Danny said, finally breaking his silence. "That won't work on me."

"Oh, it won't, huh? Hell, you're probably right. You already know what a selfish, favored, and over-privileged hypocrite you are. It comes with being you. So, how's about I direct my attention toward your dame."

"Leave Maryse out of this," Danny snarled.

"I ain't talkin' bout the French broad—who I'd fuck in a heartbeat, by the way. I'm talkin' bout your true love. The smokin' Vanessa Rodes. Tell me, does her breath taste like cherry? What's she look like naked? I guess now it doesn't matter."

"Vincent, stop it..."

Vincent was delaying the attack on purpose and even felt confident enough to talk away. It tormented Danny. The crowd started to become restless with a few shouts to "keep fighting!" and "hit him."

"It doesn't matter after the way I destroyed her," Vincent continued, ignoring the restless crowd. "She was so close to victory, just so damn close, and then I went and crushed her. Want to know why I had to beat her the way I did? It wasn't to hurt her. It was to hurt you. I wanted to see the Dragon Heart crumble in fear. I crushed her just like I did Peter. Just like I did every fighter in this tournament. I wanted you to know that you put all of them in the hospital. Their suffering was because of you. You scarred me, you betrayed me, and now, finally, after so many fuckin' years, I'm gettin' my revenge."

Danny was about to lose it. He felt his adrenaline pumping out of control. Vincent had taunted him and Vanessa for the last time. To continue to do nothing would be letting his fear take too much control, he thought. The crowd started to boo, and Vincent not attacking drove him even crazier. Vincent seemed to show no fear in letting the match go on endlessly.

"Danny, you are responsible for what happened to Peter. You are responsible for what happened to Vanessa. After this is over, and I put you in the hospital too, I'm going to take Vanessa home with me and show her what it's like to be taken care of by a real man. Vanessa Diezego has a pretty damn good ring to it, wouldn't ya say?!"

Danny's limit had been reached, and he exploded into a sprint. His anger pushed him at faster speeds than usual. He executed a bicycle kick, but Vincent leaped sideways and wrapped both fists together for a double axe handle. He swung and cracked into Danny's side. Danny felt a sharp pain as he landed on his feet. The crowd cheered the sudden flurry of action.

Danny's anger began to compound on itself. Vincent had sent nearly all of his opponents into the hospital. He had mocked Danny and mocked his loved ones. What was Vincent's punishment for it? Victory.

Danny threw every strike he could remember at Vincent. He tried to dig deeper into his memory and latch onto the nuances. Each time he came back empty, and each time he panicked further. Whenever Danny would go for a strike, Vincent seemed to respond faster with a hit of his own. For Danny, it started to feel as if he had never trained with his father and had never fought in the tournament before. Every lesson from his father was sitting in a pile of puzzle pieces, unrecognizable. The routine continued for another minute, with Vincent landing powerful blow after powerful blow.

A flashback of previous failures ran across Danny's vision. He wondered if a rock had been placed in his head, but he knew that was impossible.

Danny struggled to get his bearings which gave Vincent time to execute a powerful uppercut into his solar plexus. The air from his body seemed to leave him all at once.

All the little tricks that made him the best and gave him the edge to compete with Vincent were like a blur in his memories. He knew they existed, but they were put away in a lock box he could not open.

In the heat of the fight and filled with growing panic, he remembered the doctor telling him he had to let go and let himself remember. He remembered Vanessa saying it to him as well, over and over again. Neither of those memories helped unleash the old ones.

Danny's jaw hung open while he tried to get rid of the knots in his stomach. Vincent leaped into the air executing a spinning front kick to Danny's head. The impact sent Danny onto his back. When

Danny opened his eyes, he was surprised to be looking at the lights on the ceiling. He wondered if the fight was over already. If he'd lost.

Seeing Vincent jumping into the air with his foot extended gave him his answer. Danny's instincts took over, and he found himself rolling out of the way just in time. He got back to his feet and zipped a vicious roundhouse toward Vincent's chest. It connected with a sickening smack. Danny dropped down for a low roundhouse kick with his other leg and hit Vincent's shin. Vincent's body jerked sideways.

Danny knew this was his last chance to come back. The aches and pains in his body were starting to grow beyond what he could control in his mental state. Danny followed up with another roundhouse to Vincent's hamstring, another kick to his side, and then a kick to the rib cage. Each connected at lightning speed with matching damage.

Danny executed a spinning hook kick as Vincent screamed, "Go to hell, Richmond!" while rocketing his fist forward.

Like a bulldozer blowing through a wall, Vincent's fist slammed into Danny's chest. Danny felt a tremendous pain build as his breathing turned into sporadic gasps. His leg wobbled till his foot hit the ground. His head jerked with each breath he took. The tweezer-like pain in his ribcage became compounded by the heavy constricting in his chest.

His fear had skyrocketed beyond control. Danny knew Vincent hit him with his patented chest punch, and it only drove his mind into a bigger frenzy. He was losing.

Vanessa watched Danny's poker face crumble. *Oh my God, no. Not this way. Danny, you can't lose...*

She could see the sheer panic taking over his psyche. She knew Vincent could see it too.

Vincent smiled, "And there it is! The fear that I crave! Let it eat you alive, you pathetic piece of trash!"

Vincent shot his first forward again for another chest punch. Danny threw his hand out to block the strike and felt an excruciating lightning bolt run up his arm. Vincent executed a roundhouse kick to Danny's ribcage and then again to the opposite side. Danny was teetering with his entire body inflamed. His mind could not slow down to concentrate.

Vincent rocketed a straight kick to Danny's shin, collapsing him to one knee. Vincent arched his elbow back and snapped his fist forward. Danny didn't have time to blink before he felt Vincent's rock-like fist pound into his temple. Stars exploded across his vision, and he felt his body become weightless. His head wobbled back and forth while his body twirled to the ground.

For Danny, time seemed to move in slow motion. The lights in the amphitheater glared brighter than ever. The noise of the crowd came through like a jumbled radio message. The feeling in his body repeatedly vanished and returned. He could feel his stomach against the platform. The platform left a cool feeling on his cheek.

The sensation was familiar. He had felt the same way the last time he had fought Vincent.

He could remember how Vincent's final blow felt. He could remember the anxiety, relief, and humiliation while falling off the platform. His mind brought him back to Selena, reassuring him after the fight. It was a memory that he had lost after his accident. That memory led to another lost memory with Vincent, Selena, and him on a mission together.

The dots began to connect one after the other, picking up speed as they went. The images and conversations coming back in chapters suddenly burst to life. The cages repressing his memories crumbled under the pressure of the moment. Suddenly it all came back in a waterfall of memories as if they had always been there.

He remembered training with his father for the very first time at the age of five. He recalled the feeling of his first green belt being tied neatly around his youthful waist and the happiness it brought him. He remembered every mission and every little detail he once knew. All of the martial arts battles returned. He could hear his opponents and see their attacks. He could feel what he felt in those moments. He remembered throwing his first roundhouse kicks with Vincent by his side. His graduation from the Marine Corps Boot Camp with Vincent and their brotherly bond happened right in front of him. He remembered his first meeting with Vanessa and the love at first sight that transpired.

He could still hear her beautiful voice and see her bright smile, "Hi, I'm Vanessa Rodes."

He was eighteen, and he leaned backward with his father's fist missing him by centimeters. It was the first fight where he had gained the upper hand on Thomas, even if only for a moment. He embraced his father in a powerful hug. Their training sessions always ended in a father-son hug for him and Vincent.

His father said to him, "When your mind tells you there is nothing left in the tank, that means you have another few miles left to go."

One last memory came back, bringing him an explosion of confidence.

He remembered his father's words that he repeated to him whenever he felt lost, "Danny, listen to me… The heart of a true warrior rests not with his number of victories but with his courage and honor. You are a lethal weapon in the arsenal of democracy. You fight for honor, respect, and, most of all, for the innocent. You must believe in yourself and stay true to your morals. You must overcome and persevere. You must remember who you are… Dragon Heart."

As this went on inside Danny's brain, Thomas sat next to Maryse, mouthing those exact words with his fist clenched.

In Danny's mind, he found himself in a dark room on both knees. Fire burst from his chest with a golden dragon racing out of him. It flew into the air and turned to stare at him. Its eyes were gold and black. Its breathing rumbled the ground beneath Danny's knees. The dragon let out a deafening roar. It raced toward Danny and flew through his flesh into his heart. An explosion of fire burst from his body as the dragon consumed his very being. Every drop of blood flowing through him felt hot. His heartbeat slowed down, and his emotions changed. The fire continued to burn as the roar of the dragon echoed from within him.

His father's words played out in his head once again, "Remember who you are… Dragon Heart."

In reality, only seconds had passed. Vincent had both fists in the air and yelled into the crowd, "He's finished! He's weak! I proved it! Now I'm going to cripple him!"

The referee was raising his finger into the air to signal a knockout victory. Danny grabbed the referee's leg. The referee's eyes widened, and he brought his hand down.

Danny placed both elbows underneath him and slowly rose to his feet. Vincent turned, and his smirk disappeared. Danny got into his fighter stance and stared Vincent in the eyes. A smirk grew on Danny's face as he stood with his feet planted steadily against the platform. His adrenaline was nullifying his pains.

Thomas leaned into Maryse with a glow on his face and pointed, "Ya' see that smile, Maryse? That's the smile Dragon Heart gets just before he's about to engage in an epic battle. He's back. Just like I knew he'd be."

Vincent noticed the change immediately, "Well, well… It looks like Dragon Heart wanted to join the fight after all. Welcome back."

They began to circle each other and eye the other like prey. They were on opposite ends of the platform, the twenty-four-foot distance between them looming. Danny inched a step forward. His breathing was relaxed, and he had honed in on Vincent. The crowd around him was reduced to quiet background noise. Danny was so focused that he noticed Vincent's every action, from the sweat running down his face to the time between each breath to the angle of his body as he feinted a punch.

Danny inched a step closer, and Vincent sprinted forward while screaming at the top of his lungs. It was psychological warfare, and Danny could hear his scream like a lion roaring. Vincent leaped into the air shooting out his heel like a spear. Danny swiftly rolled forward, and it sent Vincent flying over him. He came out of his roll as Vincent landed on his feet. Vincent swung in a circle with a spinning heel kick. Danny lurched into the air and flipped. Vincent's kick swung past its target, and he barely had time to look up as Danny shot his leg backward in mid-air. His heel smacked into Vincent's temple. The friction sliced Vincent's skin leaving a red stream of blood.

Danny landed with his back to Vincent, who capitalized with a powerful sidekick. Danny turned his body and felt the kick indent into his stomach. Danny executed a posthaste thrust kick that struck Vincent in the same area. Vincent responded with a straight punch, and Danny knocked it away. Danny responded with an uppercut, and Vincent chopped it back. Danny attempted a roundhouse, and Vincent kicked it away. Vincent attempted an axe kick, and Danny pushed it down with both hands. They both struck at lightning speeds and deflected all the same.

The speed picked up as the exchange of reversals continued. Back and forth they went, striking and countering, parrying and dodging each other in almost perfect symmetry. Their exchange seemed like it might go on forever when both men, suddenly inspired by the same impulse, lurched into the air at the same moment, each landing kicks on each other that left both men on the ground.

They both kip-upped to their feet and swung around with their fists out. Their fists flew over the other. Danny's cracked into Vincent's head as Vincent's cracked into Danny's. Danny's fist made contact with the open wound, which splattered blood from Vincent's brow, leaving his face covered in a crimson mask. Vincent's knuckle dug into Danny's eyebrow and sliced through the flesh.

They both swung their leg upwards. Their heels collided into each other. A wave of pain shot up both of them as they stepped backward to recompose themselves. The small break in action gave way to thunderous applause from the audience. The energy in the room had kicked into high gear. They were both operating at 100 percent, and from the crowd's point of view, they were equals. This added an organic layer of excitement that had everyone leaning on the edge of their seat.

Vanessa had her fist clenched, and she could no longer hide her expression as she shouted, "Fuck yes! Come on, Danny, kick his ass!"

Thomas said to Maryse, "This is what this tournament is about!"

Danny was left with vision in only one eye as the other was caked with his blood. His face, like Vincent's, was blanketed red. Danny wiped the blood from his sight. Vincent's attack had been calculated and wise. Busting him open in that spot would guarantee vision problems throughout the fight. Danny respected the move from his deadliest rival.

Danny paid attention to Vincent's chest. It rose a little higher, and his breathing seemed to be a little faster. Vincent's arms and head were also slouched. Danny let his eye glance at the time clock for a split second. He was beyond the time of Vanessa's fight. He knew what he had to do.

Danny did not waste time circling. He rapidly flanked Vincent in a few large steps and swung for a straight punch. Vincent easily knocked it away with his forearm. Danny responded with a punch from the opposite arm, and Vincent knocked it away. Vincent responded with a low roundhouse kick. Danny lifted his leg, and Vincent's shin cracked into his calf. Danny exaggerated his pain and yelped while tilting to the side.

Vincent zipped another roundhouse kick aimed at Danny's side. Danny flipped through the air and landed behind Vincent. Danny initiated a swift sidekick that slammed into Vincent's lower back. Vincent felt as if a brick wretched through the area of impact. Danny repeated the same kick with the same effect. Vincent spun around to protect his injury. He felt the sensation of buzzsaws dancing across his back. It was sharp and debilitating.

Danny could see Vincent struggling to mask his pain. Vincent attempted another roundhouse kick aimed at Danny's knee.

For Danny and Vincent, it played out in slow motion. Danny knocked Vincent's attack away with his forearm while engaging in a rocket launcher punch of his own. His fist crashed into Vincent's chest like a boulder through a wall. Vincent's heavy breathing deteriorated into giant gasps of air. Each breath he took was met with the pains of a bruised lung. Each movement gave way to the buzz saws in Vincent's lower back. Vincent's ego could not stand the idea of his own attack being used against him.

Danny could see the look of fury in Vincent's eyes. Vincent's head jerked with each struggled breath. Vincent's arms were wobbling, and his stance was weak. Danny felt the momentum shift to his side, and his confidence rose.

Vincent snapped a lower roundhouse kick at Danny because it was the least painful to his back. Danny leaped into the air and shot a punch into Vincent's nose. Vincent felt a snap as blood spurted from his nostrils. The injury immediately forced tears to uncontrollably fill his eyes, blinding his vision.

Danny got into his fighter stance and connected with a lower roundhouse kick to Vincent's ankle. Vincent's body tilted, and Danny executed a straight punch with shotgun power. It blasted into Vincent's shoulder, and he felt a pop. The crowd gasped at the noise, and Vincent felt the numbing sensation of a dislocated shoulder. His arm dangled back and forth, useless.

Danny moved at cat-like speed and landed a trio of roundhouse kicks to Vincent's hamstring, and it forced his body to buckle on one side.

Vincent held himself up with one foot while throwing a punch of desperation. Danny caught it and pulled him forward. He shot a sideways kick that smashed into Vincent's head. Vincent's staggered backward.

Danny continued with his volley of roundhouse kicks. He smashed multiple hits into Vincent's calves, hamstrings, sides, and chest. Each strike was a crushing blow to Vincent's confidence. Blood and involuntary tears blinded his vision. Pain consumed his entire body. He had one fist in front of him while the other arm dangled. He felt Danny's shin snap against his dislocated shoulder and then Danny's other shin snap against his head.

Vincent's eyesight turned to black for a split second. He fought back unconsciousness in time to see Danny staring directly into his eyes. Vincent returned eye contact. It only lasted a second but felt like an eternity for both. Their pasts and everything that led them to this moment flashed before their eyes. Danny knew he was where he was supposed to be. Vincent was in disarray and dreadful.

Danny pushed both feet into the platform and leaped high into the air for a spin kick. He came around full circle, and his heel smacked into Vincent's temple. Vincent's head wobbled back and forth while his body twirled to the ground. For Vincent, the noise of the crowd became nothing, and his vision turned to black. His body fell flat onto the platform, with his head bouncing off of it.

Danny landed on his feet while the referee rushed in to check on Vincent. The referee threw his finger into the air, pointing at the judges. The gongs of victory began to echo throughout the amphitheater as Danny collapsed to both knees with his fist clenched by his sides.

The crowd exploded from their seats with thunderous applause and deafening cheers.

Vanessa sprang up from her seat, ignoring the pain in her ankle as she pumped her fist, "Fuck yes! He did it! He did it! He fuckin' defeated Vincent!"

Blood covered Danny's face and chest. His eyes were watery from pride and joy. He felt an eruption of adrenaline and confidence run through him.

On his knees with the gongs of victory still sounding and the crowd roaring, he shouted at the top of his lungs like a war cry, "Yyyyeaaaaaaaaaaa!"

His head wavered with each breath he took. He felt strong, he felt confident, and he felt the heart of a dragon beating in his chest. He knew who he was, and he was reminded of his purpose. The impossible comeback did not seem so impossible anymore. Danny Richmond had defeated Vincent Diezego. Dragon Heart had overcome and persevered.

The crowd moved about the amphitheater, still in awe of what they witnessed. Danny held a blood-stained rag against his head. Georgio and Danny exchanged a firm handshake.

Georgio said, "That was tremendous, Mr. Richmond. Simply tremendous. That was one of the best fights I have ever seen."

Danny replied, "Thank you, Mr. Moroder, that means a lot. It really does."

"Daniel! My Daniel!" Maryse called out with a shout.

He prepared for another slap. She hugged him and kissed him on his bloody face. He smiled in relief but was surprised when she grabbed him by the arm and began to pull.

"What is it, Maryse?"

"There is someone you must see!"

"Who?"

Maryse pulled Danny back to her seat and found only strangers talking amongst themselves. Her eyes narrowed, and she looked everywhere.

Danny gently placed his hand on her shoulder, which finally halted her. He smiled, "Okay, what is it? Who did you want me to see? These people? Are they fans?"

Maryse stomped the floor, "What? No... Daniel. Your father. He was here to watch your fight."

Danny's smile disappeared, "My father? Maryse, my father died twenty years ago..."

Maryse shook her head, "What? Are you mad? Thomas Richmond was just here. He was talking to me. During the fight, he said some words like fight, honor, and respect. Arsenal of democracy and remember who you are, Dragon Heart."

Danny's heart sank. Remembering his father's words verbatim again would have been a more special moment if he was not so confused, "How did you know his name was Thomas? I've never talked about him with you."

"Because he introduced himself to me!"

Vanessa hobbled toward Danny and called out to him. Peter followed behind her. He welcomed the distraction and turned to them.

Peter high-fived him, "Now that is how you whoop some ass!" He spoke at rapid speed with equal excitement, "My God, that was the greatest fight I have ever seen! Way to teach that jerk a lesson!"

Danny laughed, "At this point, I'm convinced you're more excited about this than I am!"

"You kiddin'?" Peter said. "I plan to never let that punk live this loss down! That'll teach 'em to break my elbow. You should be so proud of yourself, brother. You did it."

Peter paused and looked to Vanessa, "By the way. I was right. This tournament was a good idea, after all!"

They all looked at Peter, squinting. Danny had patches of blood caked on his chest. Vanessa was in a sling and an ankle brace. Peter was in a tight cast.

Maryse shook her head, "My god. All three of you need to be committed."

They all broke out into laughter. Peter walked up to Maryse and didn't allow himself time to breathe as he raved to her about why his plan had worked out great after all.

Vanessa walked up to Danny. They embraced in a careful and long hug. They slowly released, and she spoke, "That was fuckin' awesome. You did it. Dragon Heart is back, ah?"

Danny gave a light smile, "Yea, I guess so. Thank you for having my back."

Vanessa shrugged, "I owe you, big time. Even so, it was my intention to win. Trust me, one day I'll win this tournament and take your championship."

They both smiled big. Danny knew it was going to happen eventually. He welcomed the challenge from her. Danny observed the amphitheater and finally let himself soak it in. He marched into the storm and faced it head-on. He had refused to back down from Vincent. He had refused to let his mental injuries prevent him from accomplishing his dream. Even with so much work to be done, he knew he had overcome his biggest obstacle, his fears.

CHAPTER SEVENTEEN

The tournament had only ended two hours ago. A mix of blood and sweat was glistening off of Danny's body. The midnight Chicago air was cool and crisp in the parking lot. Police sirens in the distance echoed faintly, accompanied by the bustle of traffic. The streetlights were dimmed, and only the moon lit the area surrounded by towering skyscrapers. Danny threw his duffle bag into the trunk of his car and closed it shut. The nighttime had given him a much-needed taste of silence.

A pair of footsteps this late were impossible for his ears to miss. Danny turned to see Raphael walking up to him.

"Congratulations on your victory." Raphael Johnson said.

Danny leaned against the car again.

"You really are persistent, brother," Danny said.

"And you overcame your demons, it would seem," Raphael said with a genuine smile.

"My head is clearer now, yea," Danny said. It was nice to say that and mean it though he knew he still had so much to work through.

"Danny, you have achieved your goal." Raphael patted him on the shoulder. "Now will you help me achieve mine?"

"What exactly would that goal be?" Vanessa asked while limping out of the shadows with her hand to her hip.

They both turned to her. Raphael recognized where her hand was and kept his demeanor calm.

"Okay, games are over. What are you doing here?" she said.

"On a mission to save my country," Raphael said.

"Take it easy, Vanessa," Danny said with his hands out.

"Yea, fuck easy," Vanessa said. "Raphael, you're being asked by a woman with a gun. What are you doing here?"

Raphael rolled his eyes, "I don't fear you."

Vanessa said, "Fear's not the point. I would like to know how the hard drive you're carrying fell out of CIA hands and into yours."

"What?!" Danny said, his eyes widening. "Raphael, do you have what I think you have?"

Raphael reached into his coat pocket, and Vanessa placed her hand on the gun's handle.

"Slowly," Vanessa said.

Raphael nodded and pulled out the hard drive.

"Raphael Johnson." Vanessa said. "Twenty-Seven-years-old and leader of the Bassakran Resistance. You know, I had received reports that they had possibly got a trace on the hard drive and that it was with a man who had escaped Bassakru."

"That's why you're in this tournament," Raphael said.

"Originally, yes." Vanessa shrugged. "I really did enter in to protect Danny. But the agency? They gave me a directive to track down that hard drive here."

"Thanks for filling me in on it!" Danny said with a sarcastic laugh. The hard drive's presence hit Danny with a combination of suspicion and anxiety. The last time he saw it, his life was nearly ended. He always thought the situation was a sick joke. A device no bigger than the palm of his hand was worth enough to shoot him for.

"You said you didn't want any part of this, Danny," Vanessa said. "I figured the less you knew, the better. I didn't want to give you more than Vincent to worry about."

"Okay, everybody. Hold on," Danny said. "I think we're all on the same side here." Danny put his hands in the air and then looked to Raphael. "Start talking. Where and how the hell did you get that thing?"

Raphael closed his eyes for a moment and took a deep breath.

"I truly don't know." Raphael opened his eyes. "It was pure luck. We captured a high-ranking Xing official in Bassakru who had it on him. We reviewed its contents and realized we had a bargaining chip for when I came to meet you."

"So that was your plan?" Danny smirked. It wasn't clear if it was out of respect or surprise, and he didn't bother to clarify.

"What else was I supposed to do?" Raphael said. "I figured if I had something to offer you that you couldn't refuse, you'd help me."

"And you thought by harboring highly classified material wanted by the highest ranks of our intelligence agencies that you'd get my help?" Danny said.

Raphael's demeanor suddenly changed. He stared at both Danny and Vanessa as he stood up straight, "Neither of you two get it. The suffering, the death, the horrors that I and my people have been going through. My parents are dead. My brother is dead. My sister was nearly killed. Most of my childhood friends are dead! All by the hands of the Xings." Raphael continued talking at full speed, with his voice rising. "I am doing what I need to do to save my country. Somehow, I thought the Dragon Heart I heard so much about would care. Instead, I come back and find you'd rather be golfing than actually giving a damn!"

Raphael pointed at Danny. Danny felt the lingering sting of guilt as Raphael continued on. Danny could not argue against any of his points. None of that cured his suspicions of how Raphael got his hands on that device.

"You know." Vanessa left the gun in the holster and brought her hands to her sides. "You could have just come to me."

"How was I supposed to know who you are? I'm not some spy guru. I know of Danny because of stories I heard. I didn't know you were with him too."

"You want our help? Then let's start with your offer." Vanessa said.

"This cost my brother his life." Raphael handed her the hard drive, wasting no time. "Help me take the fight to the Xings."

Vanessa slid the hard drive into her left pocket.

Danny raised his eyebrows, surprised at how quickly Raphael handed it over. He took it as a sign of how genuine Raphael was.

"You gonna help him?" Danny asked her in a curious tone.

"I've tried to plead my case to upper management. Bassakru's got a real chance of beating the Xings." Vanessa said. "They're not listening to me. They might listen to you, Danny, and maybe him showing good faith by bringing this back to us will help convince them."

Danny turned to Raphael again with a new tone of voice. His eyes narrowed, and his investigative brain was on, "You found that thing off of a high-ranking Xing official? Who?"

"His name was —"

Raphael was cut off by the sound of a bullet being loaded into the chamber of a pistol. The tense conversation had blinded all of them to the three men who had positioned themselves strategically around the parking lot. All three Xings were armed with a gun, and all three had red Xs tattooed on their knuckles.

Danny and Vanessa immediately recognized the one in the center.

Lin John smirked, "Well, look at this. After all this time, it's led me right back to you two."

"How the fuck?" Vanessa said.

"Thank you, Mr. Johnson," Lin said. "For not only leading me to the hard drive but to these two scum bags. Hand over the device, or you'll all die."

A part of Lin's face was scarred with lumps and pinkish flesh. They were permanent burn wounds received from the plane's explosion. The LED lights reflected off of his damaged skin.

Vanessa removed the hard drive from her right pocket, and Lin snatched it from her hand. He placed it into his coat with a sigh of relief.

"You two created the freak show before you. I'd have preferred you killed me, but instead, I live. Now you'll pay the consequence." Lin said.

"Fuck you," Danny said to him. Danny didn't bother to get anxious because he knew he had to stay calm. Looking at Lin's scars, Danny knew he wasn't the only one wounded by that mission.

"I wondered," Lin said. "How long I would have to sit through those barbaric fights until I finally found who I was looking for."

Peter's steps were loud and raved with the excitement of a schoolchild, "Oh my God, Danny, that was fucking incredible! Let's go get some food! What a fucking vic—" Peter's jaw dropped, and he froze in place. "Holy shit! Guns! How? Who?"

Lin and his soldiers turned for a split second. Vanessa pulled out her gun, and they immediately turned to aim at her. Vanessa's pistol had a suppressor attached to the gun barrel, and she aimed it at Lin John's head.

Fuck. Danny thought to himself. Vanessa didn't have time to pull the trigger.

Lin's henchmen, Yan and Nicky, had their guns aimed at Danny and Raphael. Vanessa recognized Nicky as being one of the muggers from a week earlier.

"Danny. What the fuck is going on?!" Peter shouted.

Danny put his hand up, "Peter, big daddy, it's work stuff. Just go, please."

"Work stuff?! Okay, where do you work?!" Peter said. "I'm not buying that State Department bullshit anymore! State Department employees don't get into Mexican stand-offs outside of a bingo hall in the middle of Chicago, I don't give a fuck how long they've been there!"

"Please." Lin gulped with his hand trembling. "Stop talking before we make you a target!"

"Stop talking?!" Peter screamed in a frantic state. "There are fucking guns pointed everywhere! Welcome to Chicago! Shit!"

Lin and his comrades could not take their eyes off Vanessa, who stared back at them. Danny noticed their concentration immediately. Vanessa was known as the fastest gun in the west for a reason. They all knew that nobody had ever been in a one-on-one gunfight with her and lived to talk about it.

"We have three guns to your one, Vanessa. Don't even try it." Lin said, forcing his concentration.

"Oh, and you can count?" Vanessa said with a shrug

"Fuck counting!" Peter screamed even louder, with his head shaking with each word. "Will you guys please put down the guns! It's just a damn martial arts tournament, for Christ's sake! Don't like the results? Then just come back next year! Enter it yourself like I did! It worked out well for me! Except the elbow, of course!"

Peter continued rambling in a frantic hysteria. The seconds blended into a minute as Lin John bit his lip and sweat beaded down his face. His efforts to keep his eyes locked on Vanessa were clearly slipping as Peter grew louder and more frightened.

"Please stop talking!" Lin shouted while staring at Vanessa. Peter kept raging on anyways.

The back and forth between Lin and Peter repeated endlessly, with Lin's request being ignored by Peter each time. The routine had gone on for another minute. Vanessa and Danny appeared extremely calm. Raphael was motionless, observing the situation in silence.

Peter's voice raised to a high pitch as Lin's eyelids twitched with frustration.

"Oh please! Please!" Lin screamed at the top of his lungs while turning to Peter. "Just shut the fuck up already! Shut. The. Fuck. Up!"

Lin's head was turned, and his comrades Yan and Nicky turned for a split second out of panic. Vanessa's eyes narrowed, and she pulled on the trigger. Nicky turned back to be greeted by her bullet. His body fell backward while Danny and Raphael leaped forward. Danny grabbed Lin's hand and aimed it away from Peter. Raphael kicked the gun out of Yan's hand and tackled him to the ground. Vanessa had decided to shoot Nicky first to stop him from shooting Danny.

Lin went to fire his weapon on reflex, and Danny chopped his forearm. Lin's gun hit the floor and was kicked far across the ground in the ongoing scuffle.

Lin threw a rear heel kick at Danny. Danny instinctively checked the kick with his shin but was so exhausted from his battle with Vincent that the force knocked him back. Danny gasped as Lin elbowed him and charged toward the entrance to the building for his gun.

Vanessa dropped to one knee and aimed at Lin, preparing to fire, but Peter rushed over to help Danny and prevented Vanessa from getting a clean shot.

Yan kicked Raphael off of him and rushed to his feet. It stole Vanessa's concentration, who aimed and fired two shots at him. Yan collapsed.

Vanessa aimed back at Lin and found Peter still in the way.

"Peter! Move!" Vanessa shouted. Her ankle prevented her from sprinting after him.

The door swung open from the other side. Holding a rag to his head and stretching his shoulder, Vincent Diezego stepped out with a lit cigarette in his mouth. Lin smacked against Vincent, and Lin collapsed to the ground with the hard drive sliding through the alley. Vincent was covered in bruises and looked ready to pass out. Looking at the chaos, he squinted and caught the tattoos on Lin's knuckles.

Lin rushed to his feet and reached for his pistol, which was within grabbing distance. Vincent swung forward, and his fist crashed into Lin's chest full force. Lin gasped and yelped as his body fell into a puddle. Vincent kicked the gun in the opposite direction.

Lin grabbed the hard drive and used a nearby dumpster to scramble to his feet. His head bopped with each breath as his chest constricted. He sprinted off as fast as he could, eventually turning onto the street and disappearing.

Vincent reached down for his rag and placed it back against his head. He took a drag of his cigarette and walked toward his car. He nonchalantly stepped over the two dead Xing without a hint of emotion. There were now only the sounds of the city in the distance.

"Thanks for helping us back there," Danny said, trying to hold back his smile.

Vincent stared at him for what seemed like an eternity, removed the cigarette from his mouth, and then finally said, "Go fuck yourself."

Vincent popped his trunk and placed his duffle bag in it.

"But-But you helped us..." Peter said, oblivious.

Danny said nothing, already understanding everything by the look on Vincent's face. Vanessa and Raphael clearly understood too.

"Can it, Peter," Vincent said as he turned to Danny. "I didn't do it to help you people. He was going for his gun, and besides, the Xings are a bunch of fuckin' assholes. Now get the hell outta my face."

Vincent got into the driver seat of his car, and soon enough, he had driven away.

Raphael placed his hands over his head and was clearly panicked.

"Lin got away with the hard drive," Raphael said.

Vanessa put her gun away and reached into her left pocket, pulling out a hard drive.

Danny and Raphael shared a look.

"Truthfully, Raphael," Vanessa said, "My plan was to steal the hard drive from you and replace it with a phony so that you'd never know. You didn't think I banked on some resistance from those jerks?"

Raphael did not smile, but his look of dread seemed to relax. Danny took another deep breath. He had finally defeated Vincent and allowed himself to remember. He had two hours of peace before the chaos resumed. He had all he could take for the rest of the night.

"Enough of this," Danny said. "Vanessa, you need to call whoever your current liaison is and get them to clean up this mess. And Raphael, you need to get yourself protection. I'm going to get Peter out of here so he can stop pacing, and then I'm going to call Maryse to make sure she is okay. She took a taxi home to get away. None of us are going to tell her what happened."

"I'm gonna stay and speak to Raphael." Vanessa turned to Raphael. "Stay with me for a while longer here. We'll talk. I can't promise you anything, but I promise I'll try."

Raphael kept his expectations low, and his expression showed as much, "One tree can't fill a forest. I will take any help I can get."

Raphael and Vanessa continued to chat away while Danny grabbed onto Peter, who was still pacing and rambling. Danny guided him to his car and opened the passenger door for him.

Danny had not taken the time to even react to the situation. His decades of training taught him survival depended on a clear head. The pain would come back to hit him days later when he was out of danger, but for now, all he could do was stay focused.

Danny was stuck at a crossroads. Did he follow Vanessa and Raphael on this hot trail? Did he go after Lin John? He wasn't sure if he was ready to make any of those decisions. All he knew was that for the first time in a long time, he had a purpose again.

CHAPTER EIGHTEEN

The thought of being sidelined for another month enraged Vanessa, but the agency was not budging. Until her injuries healed, she was on medical leave. Vanessa walked through the Art Institute of Chicago, trying to calm her mind.

Danny and Maryse were up ahead, enjoying the beautiful art.

"You doin' okay?" Danny turned back to ask Vanessa.

She nodded with a polite smile. She was happy to see Danny happy. He was a lot more of his old self than before. She could tell by the way he carried himself he was ready for battle at any moment. She wondered if that meant he would be prepared for field work again too.

Vanessa kept her eyes everywhere; on the environment, her associates, and the people all around her. She had just gunned down two Xings a few nights ago, and Lin John was on the run. Surely the Xing Empire would have something to say about it now that they knew who she was.

Danny and Maryse were in mid-laughter observing a unique painting. Vanessa could not help but be pulled in. Maybe for one night she could turn her brain off and enjoy herself.

"I always love coming here. There's always something crazy to see!" Vanessa said. She turned her head sideways to get a different perspective of the painting. As she did, she heard a familiar voice.

"And just what do we have here?!" Robert Puerto said as he danced around with excitement. Danny and Maryse turned to greet him. Danny laughed again and shook his head.

"Who are you?" Maryse asked with a squint.

Robert put his hands in the air, "Just a worker at this museum here and a really big fan of the Golden Dragon Tournament! Badass fighting you two!"

"The fights leaked that quickly? Wow," Danny said, playing along with Robert's performance.

Vanessa scratched her eyebrow while trying to contain her laughter. Robert had to be here on business, and yet Maryse would never know it by his fanboy gimmick.

Danny stepped closer to Robert, "How you been, brother?"

The three of them shared a hug.

Robert took a glance at Danny as if sizing him up.

"You look healthier than you have in a little bit," Robert said. "I'm thrilled to see that. Are you doing alright?"

Danny had worked with Robert many times but had not spoken to him since his accident. Vanessa rarely ever went on a mission without reading an intelligence briefing prepared by Robert.

"Thankfully, I'm starting to feel better. Long way to go, though." Danny said honestly.

"Well," Robert said while pulling out his phone. "As a museum curator, it is my job to take photos with guests. How's about we all get together for a group photo!"

"I would love that!" Maryse said while fixing her hair.

In no time, Robert had his phone in position, and they all gathered close for a selfie. Once the photo was taken, they all stood in a circle talking.

"Great to have you back, Dragon Heart!" Robert said with genuine excitement. "That final fight! Holy hell!"

Vanessa couldn't help but smile. At least there was one other person who still recognized Danny for who he really was.

The conversation of good laughs and reminiscing continued until Maryse tugged at Danny's arm, begging him to move on to the next exhibit. Danny submitted to Maryse's request, leaving Robert and Vanessa alone near a medieval painting.

"Okay, cut the bullshit," Vanessa said, her smile fading. "What are you doing here?"

Robert paused for a moment, "Got some footage you'll want to see. Let's go for a walk."

Robert and Vanessa left the museum. They were walking through the daytime streets of downtown Chicago. The sounds of the bustling city surrounded them. Pigeons flew overhead with the smells inescapable. The warmness of the spring day made it all bearable.

"Let me see the footage," Vanessa said.

He pulled out his phone again and ran his thumbs across the screen.

"Here we go," he said.

"Xings?" she asked.

He nodded.

She felt a heaviness hit her heart. They were the looming threat that never left her mind. She only found respite from the worry for brief moments in the heat of battle during the tournament.

The video came to life with the words, "Near the city of Monrovia, Bassakru." planted across the screen. The screen faded to the actual footage. A series of tanks rumbled down the street. One tank after another rode by with a throng of Xing soldiers marching between each tank. Some of their beige uniforms were stained with mists of red. Smoke rose from the barrels of their assault rifles. The camera stayed focused on the street as the Xings marched away.

Vanessa's jaw dropped in horror, realizing what she was seeing. There were rows of bodies. The person holding the camera slowly approached, and the visual was beyond comprehension.

A voice spoke into the camera, "These are Bassakran civilians and Bassakran resistance fighters. Men, women, and children. We have called to other countries for help, and so far, no government has come to aid us in our effort. The longer you wait, the more pain we suffer, and the more the losses mount. The killings are all the same in every other Xing-occupied country. Our attempts at a unified resistance have failed to bear fruit due to our lack of communication. Many Bassakrans will die just getting this footage out of the country. We will continue to fight until the last man and never surrender. We will not stop until we are free. Your apathy is your capitulation to the Xing Empire. The Xings sphere of influence is spreading. Today it is here, tomorrow it will be your country. I pray that there are still warriors left to aid you in your battle..."

The footage cut to black.

Vanessa placed her hand over her mouth. She hated the Xings with every fiber of her being. They were evil.

Robert put his phone into his pocket, "There are more videos coming out soon. Looks like Raphael took your advice on leaking footage."

The mention of Raphael made Vanessa feel guilty, "Did he make it back okay?"

"Yea," Robert said. "He made it back."

"I should have been allowed to go with him. This is bullshit." Vanessa said.

"They'll let you back on the field once your injuries fully heal. In the meantime, they sent in somebody to help organize the resistance. He's a pretty big deal, supposedly."

"Who?" Vanessa squinted.

"I don't know who. His name is not listed in any reports. Not an accident either. I doubt even the President knows."

Vanessa knew it had to be somebody major. Time would reveal who the agency had sent on this mission.

"And the hard drive?" Vanessa asked.

"Upper management had it destroyed once and for all to prevent the information from ever leaking out again. So, you accomplished your mission." Robert said.

Vanessa did not even acknowledge her victory, "Xings are running quite the political operation. They take over countries by winning elections, break democracy while in power, and then install fascistic regimes. All that's left is an illusion of democracy. Then they have their radicals' performing acts of terrorism across the globe. You know over five countries are now Xing? They're on multiple continents."

"Xing Lei, their supreme leader, has become one of the most powerful people in the world," Robert said.

"Extremely lethal too. I've heard horror stories. Seen photos of his handy work. He terrifies me in a way no person ever has before. He's a threat to world stability." Vanessa said.

Robert and Vanessa spent the next few minutes discussing the global Xing problem. A break in the conversation gave them a moment to collect their thoughts before getting too worked up.

Robert spoke calmly, "CIA is waiting for the final status update on Danny and Vincent."

"You want the truth or what I'm going to feed them?" Vanessa sighed.,

"Truth. I'll make sure to protect Danny in whatever I report back."

"Thanks. There is no status. Danny remembers everything again. He's seeing a specialized therapist to help him cope with his trauma. He's determined to get Vincent back. No word on what Danny will decide to do after that."

"And Vincent?"

"His position is consistent: He wants us to fuck off. I can tell he disdains the Xings, but cooperation with him is unlikely. The seventh floor really doesn't have an issue with our efforts to recruit him?"

"I doubt it. However uncomfortable they would be with him, they'd bounce eventually. The problem is getting serious. Congress isn't talking about it, and it barely gets covered in the media. This apathy is a problem across the industrialized world. The Xings have ensured nobody pays too much attention anywhere."

Vanessa turned to stare at the sun shining in between the skyscrapers. In the distance, a wall cloud was closing in. There was a storm on the horizon, and she had more questions than ever.

Vincent lay in the hospital bed, staring up at the wall. His expression was blank, but it was clear his thoughts were racing.

"Why did you even come here?" Vincent asked Danny. The sounds of his vital monitors and the bustling medical staff filled the silence between them.

A single beep followed each heartbeat and each one reminded Vincent of his defeat. He was tempted to destroy the machine for his own sanity.

Danny sat in a chair next to Vincent's bed, "Just didn't recall roughing you up enough that you'd be in the hospital for a month, that's all."

"Yea," Vincent shrugged. "I may not be as hurt as I'm makin' out to be... What the fuck do you care?"

Danny stared at the wall to try and put his thoughts into words. He knew he would have to speak just right to make this conversation go in a direction that was even remotely positive.

He tapped the guard rail on Vincent's bedside. He stared at Vincent, and he felt a flood of emotions. His eyes started to water, and he used all of his training to fight back tears.

"You know." Danny barely let out. "When I was learning to walk again. I'd have this crazy fantasy you would help me through. Each time the phone rang, I thought maybe it'd be my brother to come back to my rescue."

Vincent turned his head and saw Danny's struggle, "Oh, for the love of fuck..." he let out. If he felt the same as Danny, he did not let him see it.

"We were blood brothers Vincent," Danny said.

Vincent looked away again. His lips were pressed together as he fought back his own emotions. He finally responded, "Why did you come here?'

Danny's tears almost escaped his eyes, "I want you to come home... Come back to the family. We had our battle, and we settled our differences."

"Settled?" He let out a lone and echoing chuckle. "Easy for you to say. We go a decade with no contact. No fights, no missions, nothin'. I'm on a winning streak in the Golden Dragon. I challenge you to come back so I can finally get the nightmare of you out of my head!"

"Nightmare of me? Vincent, you crushed me, and you felt the nightmare?"

"Fuck you, Danny Richmond. Fuck! You! Yea, I did crush you, except I never got to prove it. I heard about it at every single fuckin' tournament. You fell off the platform just as you were making your comeback! After what you did to me when we got back from Iran, I wanted to prove that I was the fuckin' real hero, that I was the leader. I wanted to make you pay for betraying me. And instead, I was greeted with ten years of, 'Yea, you technically won, but had Danny not tripped and fallen off the platform, he would have had you. He was coming back.' You were not coming back! No chance in fuckin' hell."

Danny's eyes were starting to swell, and he put his arms out in confusion, "That ate you alive? Of all things? Do you want to know the truth?"

"Hah! The truth, from you? Let me guess, you did what you had to do? The innocent first?"

"That moment was a nightmare for me too..." Danny paused. He found it hard to get the words out of his mouth. "I didn't fall off that platform... I dove off to save myself. I gave up."

It hurt Danny to utter those words to Vincent. He wanted his brother back by his side and if owning up to his nightmare accomplished that, then it was all worth it.

Vincent was not shocked Danny admitted to it. It's how Danny's always been, sacrificing himself for the greater good. Vincent laughed at the irony, "Guess we're two sides to the same coin, you and I, huh? Both of us living in our own nightmares, maybe even a little bit self-induced."

"Yea," Danny sighed. "We always have been. Selena always got that right about you and I."

"Hah, Selena. Jesus, if she were in this room right now. You think we're all good then, just because you were honest?"

Danny leaned forward in his chair with his hands wrapped together near his face, "Nope. Wouldn't be that stupid."

Vincent finally made eye contact with Danny, "So I had you beat fair and square in the past... All of my own wondering was for nothing. Me challenging you again for nothing. I got my ass kicked for absolutely no fucking reason! Danny Richmond, once again, is blessed with the happy ending, while I lie here in a fucking hospital bed, mentally rotting!"

Danny finally raised his voice, "Will you fucking stop it?! Why is it always competition between you and me? It never did make much sense to me, I got to be honest with ya' on that one. I had your back through and through. After all the shit we went through together, all the missions we went on. How many dictators did we topple? How many terrorists did we stop?" Danny looked to the ground and then back to Vincent as he shouted, "How many times did we save each other's lives?! Have you forgotten that?! We took bullets for each other! I love you, Vincent! Dad loved you! Mom loves you!"

He calmed himself down, "Do you realize Mom still asks about you? She wants you to come home."

Vincent's memory took him back to his graduation from Marine Boot Camp and Judith Richmond hugging him tightly. She spoke in soft, comforting tones, "I know you never felt like you had a family with your parents. It's been a tough burden for you. So, I want you to know that you will always have a home and family with us. Do you understand me? I love you, Vincent Diezego, you are my son, and I am so proud of you."

In the eyes of Thomas and Judith Richmond, Vincent was their son too. As quickly as the memory came, Vincent pushed it out of his head.

Vincent looked at Danny. Danny saw the pain in his eyes and hoped it would give way to Vincent opening his mind. Vincent stared for half a minute and then broke his silence, "So you want us working side by side again?"

Danny nodded, "Yes. But even if government work's not your bag anymore, let's just talk. Mend the fucking fence. Go out and grab a beer together. I'm tired of carrying this weight around, and I know somewhere you have to be tired of it too."

"How much you been educating yourself on the Xings?" Vincent asked.

"You know Vanessa's a point person on all things Xings," Danny said. "She's been askin' me to come back. I would feel a lot better about jumping back into the field if you were there with me. DLX is missing too, and it's possibly to do with the Xings. I know it sounds crazy, but I think it's time we put our differences aside and take up the fight against these assholes."

Once again, Vincent remained silent and let a minute pass this time. Danny wished he knew what Vincent was thinking. His poker face was strong and hid everything.

"For the last decade," Vincent said. "I've been a hitman for hire. I've been all over the world, killing asshole after asshole. My targets are all bad people. I've even got some Xing kills under my belt. You know what that means?"

Danny leaned in, curious.

"I've got plenty of blood on my hands. I've done plenty of terrible things to rid the world of terrible people. Some of the Xings I came across committed horrible atrocities. Question."

Vincent raised himself in the bed, "When you close your eyes at night to sleep, do all those sports cars, expensive suits, and gold watches silence the screams of all your victims? Do they mask their faces?"

"No, never. I hear them nightly," Danny muttered.

"Funny, isn't it. The people would call you and me heroes for our service. But deep down, we both feel like shit. We killed so many people labeled as a terrorist, so was it still murder? You ever try to work that out in your head? If who we kill are 'evil' people, does that absolve of us our sins?"

Vincent continued on that line of thought without Danny saying a word. Danny struggled with that topic every day of his life. Danny was proud of his service in protecting democracy as a Marine and an Operative. He was never proud of the kill count.

"It actually haunts me," Vincent said, regaining Danny's concentration. "I often wonder who I would be if my childhood had been different."

"I'm sorry for everything you went through," Danny said with sincerity. Danny wished he could wish away Vincent's traumatic childhood.

"Do you think you are ready, Danny?" Vincent finally asked.

Danny asked, "For?"

"To fix right your biggest regret? To face the Xings? They're far worse than you could ever imagine. The Xings are more powerful and deadly than any enemy we ever faced."

Danny wasn't sure how to respond and decided to continue with the honesty, "I don't know…"

Vincent nodded, "Do you remember our first mission?"

Danny's heart felt a million pounds wrap around it, and his shoulders sank into his chest. His anxiety made him feel like he was carrying a bag of rocks.

"Well, do you remember it?" Vincent asked more forcefully. "Y'know, with your memory problems and all."

Explosions, gunfire, and screams echoed in Danny's head. "I never forgot that, even when I was having issues. Not a day goes by where I don't think about that mission, where I don't dwell on it."

"We were young, too young to be on a mission like that. Freshly graduated from boot camp. Then we were sent off into Iraq. This was deep behind enemy lines, and as far as the record books, it never happened. We tracked down the DLX weapon to that building…"

Danny replied, "Yea, CIA recruited us for that mission. Remember how they said they saw something in us? That we reminded them of my Dad, Thomas?"

They both laughed, and there was a hint of sorrow behind it. It was the only way they could cope with the madness.

Danny continued, "The more I think about it, the more bewildering it is. God, we were even twenty years old?"

Vincent replied, "No, but we did our job. Real well. Maybe too well. We fuckin' killed everybody. The soldiers and even the scientists and secretaries... Between us gunning people down and blowing up the building, we had to have slaughtered about 300 people that night. Wouldn't you say?"

Danny remained speechless. Danny never talked about this out loud, even in his most intimate therapy sessions. For better or worse, he planned to take these scars to the grave with him. The mission hung on his conscience every single day. He never found a way to make peace for what he had done in the name of freedom.

"Wouldn't you say?! About 300?!" Vincent screamed with an echo.

Danny jumped in his seat, "Yes. Fucking 300! What the fuck is wrong with you?!"

"What about our regret?" Vincent asked as if he had not just triggered Danny. "The one mistake we made. Bringing the DLX back to our government rather than destroying it. Now it's finally come back to haunt ya, huh golden boy?"

Danny rose from his seat and began to pace the room, "We should have destroyed the weapon right then and there like we talked about. We could have just said the weapon got damaged in the building explosion. What's the worse they would have done to us? That weapon is missing now, Vincent. Somebody has it if it's not destroyed. Destroying it would have been the only thing to bring any sort of solace to that dark day."

A smile grew on Vincent's face.

"What could you possibly be smiling about, you son of a bitch?!" Danny asked.

"It's just nice to be able to remind the great Danny Richmond that no matter what you do, at the end of the day, you're a cold-blooded killer too. That look of torment on your face just makes me feel all bubbly inside."

Danny walked up to Vincent's bedside and pointed, "If you were any other man, I would kill you right now!"

He stepped back and placed his hands to his forehead.

Vincent laughed again, "Hell, you came up with the Dragon Neck Crunch that night! Maybe you can use that against the Xings!"

Danny wanted to attack Vincent in the hospital bed but restrained himself. The tears started to fight their way back into his eyes, along with the fury consuming his heart. Rather than let Vincent see any of it, he stormed out of the room. Vincent responded with loud and obnoxious laughs that echoed down the hallway. They pierced Danny's ears and followed him down the corridor like a nightmare that refused to end.

Danny marched out of the hospital and to the sports car, where Vanessa sat in the passenger seat. He opened the door and then sat down. He slammed the door shut and stared off into the night skies trying to gain control of his emotions.

"What the hell happened in there?" Vanessa asked.

"I was reaching him, I think, and then he resisted and threw it in my face. He brought up the Iraq mission…"

Vanessa knew exactly what that meant for Danny, even if he never did share the details of it with her. She knew better than to ever ask him to relive it.

Danny continued, "He also said he knows the truth about the Xings. I'm thinkin' he might even know more about the DLX. Hell, I'm thinkin' I might go in there and beat the truth out of him until he's a bloody fucking pulp!"

Vanessa placed her hand on his shoulder, "Whoa! Stop. Stop. Just relax. Don't go in there. Drive away, right now."

Danny sat in silence for half a minute fighting back his emotional impulses. He turned to Vanessa, "Promise me, no matter what happens from here, that we stick together, alright?"

"Of course. I wouldn't have it any other way."

"I have this feeling in my gut, like I did before important missions we had in the past. I have a feeling this crisis is going to get worse. We'll need to be strong for the road ahead."

He clicked his seat belt in and put the car into drive. The vehicle had smooth pick up, as always.

Vanessa said bluntly, "I've been telling you this. You ready to come back to work?"

Danny knew she was right, but there were so many parts inside of him that he couldn't understand yet. Something held him back, and deciphering it was tougher than he thought it would be.

Vanessa picked up his turmoil. She connected her phone into the vehicle and sorted through her playlist, "Where to now, Dragon Heart?"

Danny smirked, "Dragon Heart, huh? I don't know. We can just drive for a bit, I suppose."

Vanessa said, "You know Danny..."

Danny looked to her for a second and then back to the road, "What's up 'Nessa?"

"I wanted to apologize for my fuck up back in Venezuela," Vanessa said.

Danny pulled back into a parking spot.

"Okay, talk to me. What do you mean?" Danny said, leaning in close to give her his full attention.

"I've never told you this, but ever since that day of your accident. I blamed myself for it. You were retrieving the device I dropped, and then you got hit." Vanessa paused. "Yes, I was in this tournament on orders first. But once I realized you were entering, I knew I was going to do all I could to make sure it didn't happen to you again. I owed it to you after my fuck up. That's the scar I've been carrying with me lately."

Danny never broke eye contact with her and pointed at her, "Listen to me very carefully. Don't you *ever* blame yourself for what happened to me. *Ever.* It's the hazard of the job we chose. That was not your fault. It could have just as easily been you that got shot that day."

Danny reached out for a hug, and she fell into his arms. She did not cry, but Danny knew deep down she wanted to. He knew she was holding back so as to not add an additional burden on him. Vanessa was too tough for her own good sometimes. Vanessa fought the same battle with trauma as Danny and Vincent did, and yet she seemed to hold it inside differently than them.

They released the hug, and Danny continued, "You forget, but you saved my life. You dragged me out of that hell hole and got me to safety. And when I was in recovery, you were there every day."

Danny could never forget her being there in those very crucial first six months.

"I've always felt like the one who owed you," Danny said.

Vanessa took a deep breath and chuckled to relieve the tension. "Thank you. It's been a long two years for us both, I guess.'

"Yea, it has, but we're together now." Danny softly smiled.

By the look on Vanessa's face, Danny could tell a little bit of a weight had been lifted off her shoulders. He hoped she would free herself from that burden of guilt one day because she didn't deserve to carry it.

"I wanted to talk to you about something else, and I know you're committed to Maryse," Vanessa said. "I wanted you and I to acknowledge something between us. We've never really said it out loud, but we've both always known it's there."

They both knew she was talking about their feelings for each other. For a long time, they both knew how they felt but never committed. They had focused on their work and whatever partner they had at the time.

"I'm acknowledging it," Danny said.

"Thank you. I am too. That time we had apart put things into perspective for me. When I saw you again, I realized just how much I loved having you in my life. I really missed you a lot." Vanessa let herself smile.

"I missed you too." He said with a soft tone.

They let themselves sit with their emotions. They knew how each other felt, and they knew it was possible one day they could act on those feelings if they were both single. For now, their primary focus was stolen by the coming storm.

Vanessa Rodes had never stopped fighting back the darkness. Danny Richmond had, and the more he cleared his head, the more he hated his inaction. Danny had overcome Vincent Diezego and, in turn, overcame some of his own demons. He now looked to the horizon, where an even darker threat awaited. The Xing Empire.

Vanessa knew what her mission was. Danny had to decide whether he would continue his life of luxury or sacrifice it all for the lives of the innocent once again. A war was coming, and the fate of the world hung in the balance.

Made in the USA
Monee, IL
20 August 2023

41302227R00118